Twelve Stories
of Christmas

Including Five Gold Rings

Chris Brockman

D1417653

Cover design by: Art Painter

Library of Congress Control Number: 2018675309

Printed in the United States of America

This book is dedicated to adults everywhere who need a little Christmas whenever and wherever.

For we need a little music,

Need a little laughter,

Need a little singing

Ringing through the rafter,

And we need a little snappy

Happy everafter

Need a little Christmas now.

Jerry Herman

Preface

I write mostly non-fiction. In my college teaching career, I taught mostly freshman composition (essays), business writing, and such. My avocation is writing poetry. For the last six and a half years, I have written and posted an original poem weekly on my Real Poetry for Real People Facebook page. So how is it that you are about to read twelve Christmas stories by me?

Many years ago, the Detroit *Free Press* had a Sunday magazine Christmas story contest. I wrote my very first Christmas story to submit to that contest. I didn't win, but I got the bug for Christmas stories and discovered the difficulty of coming up with a fresh idea for one. That first story is included in this volume. As with all the stories herein, it has been rewritten, edited, and polished to a fine patina.

That scarcity of fresh ideas led to the writing of these twelve stories over many years. Why so long? Ideas for Christmas stories wasn't the focus of my attention throughout the years. Then, when the seed of one did appear, it had to float around my mind until it found a place to stick and germinate. It rooted through the neurons in my brain and started to grow. Whether it continued to grow and how quickly depended on the time and attention I had to tend to it. Only when one was compelling enough, did the hard work start to make it grow.

It's a truism that there are only so many literary themes. Christmas stories lend themselves especially to subsets of those themes, and it seems as if the good ones have been done spectacularly, as with O. Henry's *Gift of the Magi* or Pearl Buck's *Christmas Day in the Morning*. Nevertheless, the Christmas story bug lingered in my brain ready to seize upon a promising idea when it came into view. This resulted in more false starts than finished stories. The stories here, then, are the result of trial and error. One good thing about that is that it made me a better writer and the stories better stories.

The spread-out development of each one from the others resulted in significant variety in some aspects of length, plot, setting, and the ages and circumstances of the characters. I also made a conscious effort to vary the presentation of the stories. The final story, for instance, is in the form of a play within a story. I hope this variety makes each story and the entire collection feel fresh and rewarding.

This is not a thick book. I suggest you read one story a day, as if it were a serial in an old-fashioned magazine, and take some time to reflect upon it. Maybe just before bed would be good.

Who knows, it might result in visions of sugar plums dancing in your head.

Chris Brockman
October 1, 2021

CONTENTS

Twelve Stories of Christmas

The Goats of Christmas

Freddie and I go way back. We grew up together, literally on different sides of the church. He lived on the north side of St. Isidore's, in a ramshackle house about a mile up, and I on my family's farm on the south side, just the other side of the woods. We were best friends all through our eight years at St. Isidore's; we were even altar boys together. Funny how things turned out. We haven't spoken in years.

Freddie's home place was razed and the property sold twenty or so years ago after his mother followed his dad to an early death. My parents are gone from the area, too, but only out of state to live close to my sister. I've taken over what's left of the farm, as a gentleman farmer, while I teach at the college not far away. Freddie and I are still neighbors, but we haven't spoken to each other for years. We're still on different sides of the church.

It started after we graduated from St. I's. I went to the local high school and Freddie went off to the seminary school. I really didn't think he was serious about becoming a priest. We were both good kids, by which I mean we had our heads on straight about right and wrong, but we were also good at being kids. We had our fun; actually, we were pretty normal.

I had started thinking for myself in my last year at St. I's (a circumstance that annoyed the nuns). It seemed to me I had learned a lot more about reality and how to be a good person from my responsibilities on the farm than from teachers removed from reality and relying on a thousands of years-old book. Freddie went the opposite way. He also had struggled with the faith-as-virtue thing but decided to go whole hog over to the faith side. We had many long and amiable discussions for a while, but when he came back on vacations from the seminary, our discussion turned into arguments, which eventually grew bitter and divisive. He accused me of being not just wrong but bad; I accused him of being not just wrong but stupid. And that's where we left it.

I went away to college, and then farther away to grad school. I got married, started my family, and was doing well teaching out of state when my folks asked me if I'd like to take over the farm. This was a no brainer; my wife and son loved visiting the farm. Toddie had even stayed there for a few weeks for the previous couple of summers. I was eager to get back, myself. My folks had sold off most of the farm, including small woods that bordered St. Isidore's. What was left were the farmhouse, the big barn, and thirty acres of alfalfa. It was perfect. I had no intention of working the farm, but I had long wanted to raise a small herd of angora goats. The last pieces fell into place when an opening came up at the local college, and my wife was hired to teach at the local elementary school.

In the meantime, I had lost track of Freddie. I knew he was a parish priest somewhere. My parents had told me this, but I wasn't much interested. Our parting had been pretty bitter. I *was* mildly interested, though, and pretty surprised when the local paper ran the story that Father Frederick Preston, who had grown up here, was to be the new pastor at St. Isidore's. I'm sure Freddie knows I'm here, too, but there clearly is no motivation on either side for any sort of reconciliation.

Two years after moving back, I've started my goat herd. I have six beautiful angora females and two handsome bucks. At Christmas time, I am confident that the females are pregnant, the bucks are back in their own pen, and I look forward to kids in the spring. All is well.

***

It was with mixed emotions that I came back to St. Isidore's. My childhood had been a joy, it's true. Even though my parents didn't have much, we truly didn't need much. We had country air, and I know it's a cliche', but we had each other. That was especially important to me because they cared enough about me to come up with the tuition to send me to St. I's for school for eight years. Between this and their own personal goodness, I came to a strong moral compass that pointed away from here. Then suddenly, it turned me around and led me right back home.

But it's not the same. My parents are gone, our house is gone, and there's the thing with Todd. St. Isidore's should be filled with nothing but wonderful memories. Things don't get much better as a kid than having a school you love and your best friend no more than a mile away. New memories to be made should be equally wonderful. What a shame--and a travesty-- that he became a non-believer. With the quality of education and upbringing that boy received. . . God forgive him. His parents were good people and like second parents to me.

I can see his having doubts. . . no I can't . . . I guess I did too, so yes I can. But to turn around and insist that he's absolutely right and everything we've been brought up to believe is wrong is too much, too insufferably arrogant.

It's so funny to think that in one way we're even closer than we used to be---we're next-door neighbors--and we don't talk. You'd think he would have come to see me. I'm the one who's come home. I'm not sure what we'd talk about, if he did come, his being a professor and all. But geez, it's Christmas Eve. Maybe he'll come to mass tomorrow. Ha, fat chance.

***

"Dad!   Pan and Casper are out of their pen. I just went out to give them a Christmas treat, and they're not there."

"Oh darn, I knew that fence was sagging. I'll bet they jumped it. On Christmas Eve, too. Get the big flashlight, while I put on my coat and boots. We'll have to find them before they get hit by a car or something."

***

"Look, Dad! In this new snow you can see their tracks.

"Hey, you're right, Toddie. Are you dressed warmly? We're about to go off on a wild goat chase."

"Aw, Dad, Pan and Casper aren't wild."

"That's so, but I think the chase is going to be. Get a couple of leads out of the barn. I'll go tell Mom what we're up to, and off we go."

***

"Those crazy goats, their tracks are going into the woods. They're headed for St. Isidore's.

"Hmm . . . maybe they're going to church."

"Yeah, Dad, and maybe they think the sheep and the cow around that manger thing are real, and they're going for a visit."

"Well, I hope they make friends and stay for a while so we can catch up to them and get them back home.

***

"Oh look, Dad! There's Pan and Casper, and they're eating hay out of that manger thing. Uh oh, here comes the priest. I'll bet he's not going to be happy."

***

"Hello, Freddie."
"Todd!"
"Toddie, this is my old friend Freddie."
"Freddie, this is my son, Todd, Jr."
"I'm pleased to meet you, Mister. . . uh . . .Reverend . . ."
"I'll tell you what, Todd, Jr., you can just call me Freddie, too, if you remember not to do it when anyone else is around. What do you prefer to be called?"
"You can call me Toddie if you like, sir. Or maybe Todd, without the "junior."
"Well, Toddie, I'm pleased to meet you, as well."
"Say, Todd, Sr., don't you ever feed those goats? They seem to be awfully hungry."
"I'm afraid these two are guilty of gluttony, Freddie. They'd eat constantly if they could, and it looks as if they're especially fond of midnight snacks."
"Say, speaking of midnight, Todd, I'm saying a midnight mass in a few hours. Would you like to come?'
"Thanks for the invitation, Freddie, but that's a little late for us. But I'll tell you what, I'd like to contribute to your celebration. Your nativity scene could use some animation. Look how good Pan and

Casper there bring it alive. How about we tie them up here, out of reach of the manger so they're not eating it up, for when your congregation arrives. Toddie and I will go back and get some of our best hay for them to munch on and we'll re-stuff the manger. It's not supposed to be very cold tonight, and these goats are wearing angora sweaters."

"That's a really good idea, Todd. It's very neighborly of you. But I hope you didn't think I came out just to get your goat."

"Oh, that's a good one, Freddie. I see you haven't lost your touch. Actually, I was thinking it's time to exorcize the ghost of Christmas past and replace it with the goats of Christmas present.

Santa Claus Came to Town

Michael Jefferson suppressed a shiver and pushed his hands deeper into his coat pockets. The shiver was as much from nervous tension as it was from the frigid air. The refuge he sought in his pockets was from both.

The cool steel his hand met in his right pocket did little to mitigate the effect of the frosty atmosphere. But as his fingers wrapped around the small .22 caliber pistol there and Michael pulled his arms tight to his sides, a kind of warm glow did come over him. He'd found the gun high up in his mother's closet, but he expected it had belonged to his father. The connection created a hint of the everything's-okay feel he associated with the memory of his dad.

As Michael came to the end of the alley, the lights and the traffic resurrected his tension, and any feeling of well-being evaporated like the steam from his rapid breathing. He saw from the big clock on the façade of the department store down the block that it was still a few minutes to closing. He knew the traffic, both car and pedestrian, then, would diminish quickly to nothing. This part of the city's commercial district was in bad shape, and business was nothing like it used to be.

As the remaining shoppers exited the store, they'd pass the bell ringer in his red suit trying to importune them with a tweak of conscience. A few would drop coins and a folded bill or two into his pot. It wouldn't provide much cheer to anyone else, Michael thought, only temporarily eliminate a little misery. In his pocket, on the other hand, it could be a significant take.

The money wasn't that important in itself. He knew the amount from this location would only be a brief shower on his own financial desert. He believed, however, that it would be a step in the right direction for turning around his whole way of dealing with life. He needed to succeed in this. He needed some success in his life.

He'd thought about it, planned it out. Since his father had disappeared five years ago, when he was just ten, things had been hard—harder; they had been hard before. And he wasn't stupid. He got good grades in school, but he was street smart, too. He saw who got over in life. He saw who had money and clothes and respect. He knew he had to keep up his grades for the future, but this was for now. In the immediate, next-meal here and now, his mother could use all the help she could get—all the help he could give her. And he could use a few of the finer things in a young man's life.

His father had had strong ideas about justice, about people's getting what they deserve. He'd told his son it was wrong to take what you don't deserve. Michael had soaked up his father's values, but the fact that his father wasn't there made his authority on forceful taking less and less tenable. About deserving, Michael had long ago concluded that he didn't deserve what life was giving him. He'd decided he wasn't going to take *that* anymore. The only alternatives he could see were dealing drugs or nothing, and neither was no longer acceptable.

"Nothing" was how Michael thought of his life now—no money, no power, no status. To stay where he was, all he had to do was nothing. He'd get a job if he could, but to get a job, he'd have to wait until he was sixteen. Then he could apply for the only thing available, a fast-food job at minimum wage. Even then, he'd have to wait until a manager went through the list of those who'd applied before him. If he ever got a job, he'd have to wait for a bus to get there and then get home. Michael was tired of waiting. Waiting is nothing, too.

Then he'd found the gun. He'd never used one before, but he'd always loved playing with the toy guns his father bought for him. Christmas presents they'd been, shiny and new. They made him feel good, important, both as toys and as symbols of power. The real gun in his pocket felt familiar, as if it were new and shiny. But the power was different. He wasn't a kid anymore; he knew what a real gun could do.

The late shoppers rushed out of the stores, their adrenaline still high from the race to buy before closing. Michael killed time looking into windows down the street from his target.

People wasted no time getting on to their next task, and the street cleared of pedestrian traffic quickly. Just as quickly, Michael was next to the ersatz Santa, who was busy closing up his operation. He was turned away from Michael, and didn't see him approach, and Michael knew how to move quietly.

"Check it in, give it up, all of it!" he demanded, dropping into a semi-crouch and holding out the gun with both hands. Santa turned, and Michael found himself looking into the eyes of his father.

The effect was electric, and Michael froze. He probably would have begun pleading he was sorry and didn't really mean it, but his voice had left him. As it was, he just stared, wide-eyed, at the ebony face framed in sharp contrast by the flowing white beard.

Michael looked across years, and Santa looked back, at first stern and annoyed. Then, a smile spread over his face, oddly, considering he was looking into the muzzle of a gun.

As the realization crept over Michael that Santa only *looked like* his father, he regained some control over his body. "Give it up, the money," got out, but with little of the authority or threat of his original demand.

Santa continued smiling and softly, deliberately, began singing. "You better watch out..."

"You think I won't use this?" Michal whined. He waved the gun around, but his voice had betrayed him.

"You better not pout..."

"Shut up, you..."

"You better not cry, I'm telling you why..."

Michael felt physically ill, weak and afraid. He dropped his gun and ran off into the shadows.

"Santa Claus is coming to town."

***

Santa continued to hum to himself, and a few minutes later, the van from the mission pulled up. Two men got out and one of them asked, "Well, how'd it go tonight, William?"

"You know, collections were kind of slow, but I have another gun for you."

"Oh my god!" one of them exclaimed. "Another one? That's incredible."

"Nevertheless," William said, "I saved another one tonight."

Two Trees Are Better Than One

The new accumulation from an overnight snowfall crunched under Shelley's boots. Bright sunshine, reflected from the sparkling blanket, added to her good spirits. The coil of rope over one shoulder and the bucksaw in her other hand helped her balance as her feet sank into the snow with each step. She was on a happy mission to cut a tree for her family's Christmas.

Despite the difficulty walking the snow presented, Shelley was glad for it. The rope she brought she would tie around the trunk of the tree when she had cut it down. Then, she would loop it around her waist and the tree would slide easily across the snow, as she pulled it back to the house. The frosty whiteness, of course, also contributed to the Christmasy atmosphere.

The sky was the deep blue that only happens after an air-clearing snow covers the ground and provides a sharp contrast. Ahead were the black skeletons of the tree line that bordered her family's property. On the other side was her objective, the pines that were scattered across the back forty of the MacGregor farm.

"Farmer MacGregor," Shelley thought, and she giggled at the irony. She felt a little like Peter Rabbit. The old man would never miss one tree, but she still felt a small guilty thrill at the risk of being discovered. Mr. MacGregor had quite a reputation as a curmudgeon. He was what Shelley considered ancient—perhaps seventy—and since his wife had died five years ago, he had stopped farming altogether and had become a little reclusive. He also was known to have yelled at more than one kid who attempted to cut across his land on the old tractor path shortcut between the road in front of his house and the one that fronted hers. This included several of her friends and earned him the epithet in her circle of "Old Farmer Grouch."

Shelley stepped sideways down the side of the shallow ravine created by the natural drain between the two properties. Going back up this side dragging the tree would be her biggest challenge, but she was a farm girl, after all, though her family's farm was only six acres of hay, a large garden, and a few dozen chickens.

She had never pirated a Christmas tree before and was a little unsure of the ethics of it. She had tossed the idea around since she had gotten the inspiration to make this contribution to her family's Christmas. Money was a bit tight that year, and she wanted to do her part. Her final take on it was that the numerous trees scattered on MacGregor's farm grew wild, and nobody was using them for anything, so removing one was no big deal. There were trees on her own land, but they just weren't as nicely shaped as MacGregor's. She had done some scouting, and she knew where the best ones were.

Some of the trees on the other side of the ravine were the perfect size and shape, with nicely spaced branches perfect for hanging ornaments. She also discovered that the trees she had in mind were not visible from the MacGregor house. At least she could see only the roof of the farmhouse from there.

Shelley crunched on buoyed by the picture in her mind of how great the tree she was going to cut would look in their high-ceilinged living room. When she got to the pines, it didn't take long to pick the best one. She shoveled the snow away from its base with her gloved hands and began to saw it close to the ground. The saw was sharp, and she got about halfway through with no problem. After that, the sawing got more and more difficult. It was hard to get good leverage down low as she was, but she wanted to leave as little stump behind as possible. Her back was aching from bending over, so she knelt down in the snow, and she was able to lean against the tree and push it away from the cut, which helped a little. After a few halting inches, however, the saw would move no more, no matter how much she jerked and thrusted. Maybe, she thought, she could start from the other side. She tried to pull the blade out, but it was stuck fast.

By this time, despite the cold, she was sweating from the exertion. She fell back on the snow, her cheeks scarlet and her breath heavy. "How am I going to get this saw out," she wailed, exasperated. "I can't leave it here. And what about my beautiful tree?" The physical exertion of fighting the saw, combined with the frustration of her situation, overwhelmed her. She clasped her hands in front of her, hung her head, and started to cry.

***

"It looks like you need a little help."

The voice startled Shelley upright, and there was Old Farmer Grouch himself. He towered over her, leaving her in the most compromising position she'd ever been in.

She tried to wipe the tears from her cheeks with a gloved hand, as she scrambled to her feet. MacGregor continued, "Maybe if I pull the tree from the other side, it will free the blade. I see you have a rope. Let's loop it around the tree."

Shelley couldn't believe her ears. She was caught red handed rustling a tree, and that hand was in the cookie jar. And yet, the grinch was going to help her save Christmas. Omigosh!

"Mr. MacGregor, I'm Michelle..." But, he put up a gloved palm and interrupted, "I know who you are. We can talk about that after."

With MacGregor pulling the tree, the rest of the cut was soon accomplished, and the tree wooshed to the snowy ground. Shelley waited nervously for what came "after."

"Tie the rope around the base, and make sure you put it above a branch or two so it won't slip off."

Shelley marveled at her luck. "Mr. MacGregor, I want you to know I appreciate this."

MacGregor, whose expression had been entirely non-committal so far, frowned. "We'll see about that.

"Now, grab onto the rope, and I'll help you pull this—back to my house. I haven't put up a Christmas tree since Edna died. Since you've cut such a fine one for me, I think it's time I started again."

Shelley was aghast. "You mean we're going to drag this tree to *your* house..."

"And put it up," MacGregor finished.

***

As they came up to the house with the tree in tow, MacGregor said, "Untie the rope and cut off those two big bottom branches. I'll get some clippers to snip off the small ones." When the first twelve inches of the trunk were smooth, he pointed to the front of the house. "We can take the tree right in the front door and into the front room, but you need to take off your boots in the entranceway. There'll be enough snow on the floor from the tree without us tracking in more."

Shelley felt a little uneasy at the thought of going into the house with a man who was essentially a stranger to her, but she thought of MacGregor's age and the growing good feeling she had about him and replied, "Whatever you say."

Inside, MacGregor wasted no time. He retrieved a tree stand from the closet under the stairs, and together they wrestled the tree upright. Shelley moved it around while MacGregor sighted it straight.

"I gave most of the Christmas tree ornaments to my kids," he told her when he was satisfied with the position of the tree and had tightened it in place. "But I saved a few special ones."

He was gone upstairs for a few minutes, and Shelley looked at the family pictures around the living room, picking up one she assumed was MacGregor's wife Edna as a much younger woman. She had known her as older and only a little before she died, a few months after her family moved to their farm.

"That's my daughter," said a returning MacGregor. "Unfortunately, she lives across the country, works for some big company, and doesn't have time to get home much. Here, you can help me put some of these things on the tree."

As they hung his few ornaments, MacGregor had a story for each one—where he and his wife had gotten it or who made it, and what was going on in the family at the time. Clearly, they *were* special ornaments.

Shelley told him how sorry she was that she had tried to take one of his trees (she didn't want to use the word "steal'). He listened but didn't say anything.

When they had put on all the ornaments, the tree was still pretty bare, but MacGregor stood back and nodded approvingly. "If you want to know the best lesson of Christmas," he said, "it's that it's not what you have or what you give that's important, but what it means." Shelley thought she saw a smile starting at the corners of his mouth.

"All right, let's go get *your* tree."

They put on their boots, coats, and gloves and tromped back through the snow to the pine trees. MacGregor looked around and picked one out. "How about this one?" Shelley agreed that it was very nice, and they cut it down in short order, working as a team.

"I'll help you get it back over the ravine and up the other side," MacGregor said, and Shelley was in no position to argue. When they had gotten it up the other side, Shelley once again told MacGregor how sorry she was that she had tried to take one of his trees.

"Well, it wasn't the right thing to do, and I hate to sound trite, but if you had asked me, I would have said "Fine with me—Go ahead and cut one." But, if you learned a lesson, it's all for the better. Plus, I got a Christmas tree put up, and you got yours too. I'd say that was a good deal."

Shelley saw that little smile start again, and they wished each other a warm "Merry Christmas."

As she dragged her own special tree across the field, Shelley thought about MacGregor's budding smile and what it stood for. Her own blossomed into a beautiful flower, and she decided that there was no reason why she shouldn't go visit Mr. MacGregor once in a while. "First, though," she thought, "I'm going to call up all my friends and invite them over to make ornaments and string popcorn. I know they'll come when I tell them my story. And we'll go over and finish decorating Mr. MacGregor's very fine Christmas tree."

Silver Bells

Anna Kowalski sat on the front room sofa, carefully unpacking the carboard box perched on the straight-back chair in front of her. It was a slow process, as she took time to appreciate each item before placing it gingerly next to her on the sofa. Thanksgiving indulgence had barely subsided and she didn't have a tree yet, but she couldn't wait to check out her inventory of Christmas ornaments. It wasn't as if she didn't know exactly what she had, but she wanted to relive the story behind each ornament. So she had dug the boxes out from the closet under the front stairs.

As she held out a golden metal reindeer, she interrupted her own reverie and said out loud, "Anna Kowalski, you're acting just like a lonely old woman." Then a laugh and, "Well, if all those others can put up decorations these days right after Thanksgiving, why shouldn't I be getting ready too?" The next piece that came to hand was a braided silver rope, on which hung five exquisitely engraved silver bells. Anna got up and fetched some silver polish from under the kitchen sink and a soft cloth from the bureau drawer. She began gently to make the bells reflect clearly the sunlight coming in through the lace-curtained windows.

As she polished, she thought about Stanley and how he had worked so hard to be able to surprise her with these wonderful silver bells so many years ago. They had been expensive, and times had been lean in the years after the war. The bells were not something she and Stanley could easily afford. But what a bargain they had been. She had loved them instantly, and they had evermore been her favorite among the many other fine ornaments they had collected.

Anna finished taking the smaller boxes out of the bigger ones, put the big ones back under the stairs, and piled the others on Stanley's easy chair. Then she turned to the large, framed wedding photograph on the library table. "Stanley," she said, holding it in both hands. "You always loved Christmas so well."

She sighed and set the picture down next to the glass-domed wedding clock. Four times they'd had it fixed over sixty years, and it still kept perfect time. The chime sounded three times as she stood there, and Anna figured she'd better get busy. "This house is a mess." Anna's carefully groomed domain hadn't been anything like messy for a long time. Nevertheless, dust is relentless, and she got out her feather duster, turned on the radio to her and Stanley's favorite station, and went to work.

As Anna worked on dusting, her thoughts kept returning to Stanley and Christmas. All through the years she had wanted to give Stanley something to match the silver bells. She had given him many loving gifts, but she never thought she had approached those marvelous bells, whose light musical tinkle even seemed to be made of silver. Now she wouldn't again have the chance to give him that perfect gift.

"Oh Stanley," she sighed, and went on dusting, though after a few minutes she stopped; her spirit just wasn't in it. She went into the kitchen to make herself a cup of peppermint tea. Sitting at the kitchen table, she couldn't help thinking, as she had done for all those other years before, what she could get Stanley for Christmas.

***

Stanley's favorite things had been the radio and music. He and Anna had first connected at the wedding reception for a mutual friend of their two families. It was a Polish wedding, and they, being Polish themselves, ended up dancing polkas together. In between, they discovered they were headed for adjacent high schools, she to Detroit High School of Commerce and he to Cass Technical High School. Cass Tech had a fine music department and held great dances. They went to dances and concerts together at Cass Tech through high school, started going steady, and got married not long after graduation. They opted for jobs instead of college and never regretted it.

They scrimped and saved from Stanley's job at the Cadillac Assembly plant and hers, before the children started coming, as a bookkeeper downtown in the David Whitney Building. As soon as they could, they bought a Philco console radio as their first major purchase. They were so proud of it--over four feet high! She polished its beautiful walnut cabinet faithfully, just as faithfully as Stanley sat in front of it in his big oak rocker and pushed buttons to get their favorite stations and programs. During the war, he was fortunate in a number of ways to serve as a radio repairman. When he went back to Cadillac after the war, after GM started car production again, one of his jobs was installing radios on the assembly line.

Anna and Stanley spent many hours listening to the radio. They both were fans of big band music well into the 40's and pretty much rued the advent of guitar and drum rock and roll. Their favorite station had long been WJR, the Great Voice of the Great Lakes, which played a mix of middle-of-the road popular music. In 1959, WJR began *Adventures in Good Music,* an hour of classical music with the accessible and informative analysis of Karl Haas. He and Anna loved it and listened regularly before he left for work on the afternoon shift. Anna still polished the big Philco Radio, though its walnut veneer was peeling in a few places. They had continued to listen to it through the 50's, but when parts began to get hard to come by and with the advent of FM, they had finally given up and bought a good AM-FM set. They put it on top of the Philco so they could still sit in front of the big radio and listen.

They discovered full-time classical music on a Detroit public radio station, and classical became the background music of their lives. When this station switched to a jazz format and then a news/talk format, Stanley and Anna also switched to Toledo public radio, which still broadcast classical full time. Stanley's favorites, all good Poles, were Chopin, Wieniawski, and Paderewski. He read about their lives and called in to request programs to request his favorite pieces. They contributed what they could to station fundraisers over the years. In the past five years, it had gotten less and less as Stanley's medical bills had mounted.

Their children had started to help them out financially, but more, they had helped by not pestering them to move out of their old house in the old neighborhood. Good kids, they understood what it meant to their parents to stay where they felt was home, even if the neighborhood was going downhill. They had brought up moving a few times, but Anna and Stanley (most recently Anna alone) had patiently explained why they weren't going anywhere. The kids had to be satisfied with admonishing Anna to please be careful.

Anna sipped her tea, wandering through thoughts of Christmas and Stanley. On the radio in the other room, a waltz by Tchaikovsky had just finished and the announcer was saying, "Today's programming is brought to you through the generosity of Dr. Paul and Emily Carter in honor of the thirteenth birthday of their daughter Elaine."

Slowly, this filtered into Anna's reverie, and a smile spread over her face. That's it!" Stanley had loved music and would have loved to have been a musician and bring it to others. That was one of the reasons they had contributed to public radio; it was one way of making music happen. She went over to the telephone and called the radio station. She connected with the program director and told her what she wanted to do. For $120, she could have a 15-scond spot at the beginning of a particular program, dedicate it to Stanley and choose a piece of music. Miraculously, no one had yet reserved that spot on Christmas Day.

Anna's problem of a Christmas present for Stanley was half solved. She knew *what* to get; now she had to figure out how to pay for it. She could ask her children for the money, but she wanted to do this herself. This was going to be her silver bells.

She put her teacup into the sink and walked into the front room. She opened one of the small boxes on Stanley's chair and took out the silver bells. She shook them once and smiled at their sweet jingle and put them into her purse. Elias Stopsinski's pawn shop was eight blocks away. She'd have to hurry to get there and back before it was getting dark. She put on her walking shoes, went to the closet for her coat and an umbrella, and went out.

Stopsisnki was an old friend, and his shop had been in the same place for thirty-five years. She and Stanley had stopped in occasionally over the years and had even used his services a few times. Anna hadn't seen him, however, since Stanley's funeral. Appropriately, Anna thought, the shop bells rang cheerily as she entered the store. "Hello. Anna," Stopsinski greeted her. "It's been a while. How are you getting along?"

"I'm okay, Elias, but you know I miss Stanley terribly." She wasn't ready to share the meaning of her mission yet, but she took the bells from her purse and asked him what he could give for them.

Allaying his curiosity, Stopsinski examined the bells carefully and weighed them. "I'll give you my best, Anna, because you're a friend. The best I can do is $90." Anna, still aglow with inspiration, explained her plan to Stopsinski. She never stopped smiling as he handed over $120. She invited him to listen if he could on Christmas morning. "Stanley won't be there in person, but he'll be listening too."

"For heaven's sake, be careful with that money," Stopsinski admonished her. Maybe you should call a cab."

"No need, Elias. It's only eight blocks. I'll be fine. Alicia's coming over tomorrow, and I'll have her take me to the bank."

***

The light rain that had been falling had stopped as she left the pawn shop, so Anna didn't need to put up her umbrella. It was a gray day, nonetheless, and there were few people out, even on the main street, really just one young man on the other side. As she turned onto the street into the neighborhood and began walking, the man stopped and looked both ways, waiting for traffic to clear.

About halfway down the first block, Anna turned instinctively to check behind her and saw another person starting down the street. She was in good shape and walked whenever she could, and she felt safe in her own neighborhood. She didn't walk fast, however, and though she felt a little silly about it, today she also felt a little nervous. She couldn't help turning her head slightly every dozen or so steps to check behind her. There was a man following, and he was definitely walking faster than she was. By the middle of the third block, he was close behind and she turned around sideways and stepped one foot onto the grass to let him pass.

Anna saw a young man of medium height and build, tough looking, and her heart beat fast. There had been an increasing number of old people being robbed and sometimes beaten in the city. The usual generic description of assailants fit exactly the fellow about to pass her.

It looked as if he'd pass right by, rudely ignoring her, scowling straight ahead. But he turned suddenly and with, "Gimme the purse, grandma," grabbed her purse. Anna held on with all her might. There was no way she'd let this thug have his way. But with both of them tugging it, the purse came open and the $120 fell out in a wad. Her far more nimble attacker bent over to pick it up, and Anna saw Stanley's present flying away.

Anna had never been particularly self-assertive. She came from a period and class that defined the home as the woman's place and the man as the provider. She had made a comfortable home for Stanley, and Stanley had taken care of her. It was an arrangement of mutual convenience. She had never relinquished her value as a person, and Stanley had never expected her to. She hadn't been the "little woman" but a real partner. She never thought of herself as weak or timid, so she'd had few practical problems since Stanley died.

As the purse snatcher bent over, something came alive in Anna that she'd never felt before--rage. She shifted her umbrella to her right hand, clutched it in the middle, and brought its heavy carved handle down as hard as she could on the back of the young man's head. He crumbled at her feet, but she was still grateful when a police cruiser turned onto the street. It stopped next to her with a small screech. "Neighbor called and said you were having some trouble, ma'am. Thank heavens for nosy neighbors, huh?"

The adrenaline or whatever that had powered Anna's outburst of strength left as quickly as it came. The would-be robber began to get up, and Anna began to tremble. One of the officers grabbed him by the collar of his coat, and both officers threw him against the patrol car. Then one held him while the other frisked and cuffed.

Once the assailant had been put into the back seat, one of the officers returned to Anna. Before he could ask one question, the whole story of Stanley, the bells, Elias's pawn shop, Stanley's present, and the $120 still scattered on the ground, poured out of Anna in a cathartic stream. The officer listened respectfully before getting to the standard questions. He yelled to his partner to call another unit. As he was finishing his report, another patrol car pulled up and two officers got out.

"Assault and robbery, guys. Could you escort Mrs. Kowalski, here, home? We'll take this guy to the lockup"

* * *

Anna called the radio station the next day and made the arrangements. Afterward, she put a check for $120 into an envelope and put it into her mailbox. She didn't tell her daughter why she needed to go to the bank, but she did invite her and the rest of the family for Christmas brunch. She, of course, couldn't tell any of them of the attack. She felt better about it already anyway and decided to just let it go.

After her daughter had left that afternoon, the doorbell rang. Despite her bravado, Anna was a little apprehensive. The door was locked, however, and she could look out its window to see who was there. She saw the two police officers from the day before. She opened the door and invited them in for tea and cookies.

"We can't stay, Mrs. Kowalski. We just brought you something. We stopped in to Elias Stopinski's pawn shop—nice store he has there. He confirmed your story about the $120, and he showed us some interesting, uh, merchandise that we thought we really ought to have. Some of the officers at the precinct chipped in, and Stopinski gave us a good deal." He held out a rope chain with five highly polished silver bells.

***

On Christmas day, Anna had the radio on as she made final preparations for receiving her children and grandchildren. The Christmas cookies were stacked high, and beneath her handsomely decorated tree were handmade presents for everyone.

They all arrived together at the time she had admonished them to be there, and they congregated in the kitchen for a Christmas cookie appetizer. Anna kept her eye on the time, and just before the top of the hour, she had them all come into the living room where the radio was on, quietly concluding Benjamin Britten's *A Ceremony of Carols*. Anna turned up the sound, and after station i.d. and a promo for a program later that day, the announcer said in his rich classical voice, "Today's programming is brought to you, in part, by Anna Kowalski in memory of her late husband Stanley, who dearly loved classical music, with a special request." Out of the radio came "Silver Bells."

Five Gold Rings

D'Ondre sat in her living room contemplating Christmas and its incredible, unfortunate connection with her previous husbands. Her neat home was devoid of any decorations or symbols of Christmas. She had pledged with Xavier's death that she would not celebrate Christmas anymore, in any way. His passing had cemented in place her conviction that she was not only unlucky in love but a virtual lightning rod for her husbands' bad luck. And Christmas was the catalyst.

It had started with Kennedy, her first husband, killed coming home from work in a crash with an 18-wheeler on snow-slick roads on Christmas Eve. They had been married just one day short of two years. It was so wrong that he had to work on Christmas Eve, but he had volunteered, eager to impress his employer.

They both had good jobs, but they carried entry-level salaries. Each had big student loans to pay off and little margin for luxuries. They had agreed to a small wedding and the exchange of simple gold rings. In contrast, they had big plans after that, starting with buying the small story-and-a-half rented house, in which D'Ondre still lived. With their two salaries combined, in another year, they would have had enough for a minimum down payment. They hoped to add on to it as they started and grew a family.

Kennedy and D'Ondre had fallen in love at once with the white vinyl-sided house with a picket fence in front. Kennedy was especially impressed with the huge willow oak trees on opposite corners of the house. Their mass of foliage shaded the house in both morning and afternoon. Some of the spreading big branches even hung over the house itself. It was impossible to look up at the trees' height and spread and not be awed. They did buy the house, though D'Ondre had joked for the first of many times that if one of those trees ever came down in a storm, it would be the end of the house, for sure. It may have been a joke, but she had obtained and maintained great insurance coverage on the house, just in case.

When Kennedy died, insurance was D'Ondre's salvation. They had been paying on mortgage life insurance for only a year, but it paid off the balance owed on the house and let D'Ondre thrive on her own salary. This hardly compensated for the loss of her husband, but it made her a young widow with a paid-off house and a very eligible bachelorette.

D'Ondre met husband number two, William, ironically, at a Christmas party. For two years after Kennedy's death, she kept pretty much to herself outside of work. The main exception was Christmas when she needed to be with family. She could hardly escape the signs of the season all around her, every one of which took her back to that fateful night. But she knew the abject loneliness that would encompass her by herself, so she spent Christmas Eve, like a child, with her parents. She stayed overnight to share Christmas Day with her brothers and sisters and their children when they came over in the morning. The adults were sensitive to her feelings and acknowledged the significance of the day to her, but they deliberately tried not to be morose. The kids' exuberance filled the barrenness she would have felt alone.

D'Ondre did keep in touch with some of her long-time friends who had remained local. So it was she was persuaded to come to a seasonal party given by her friend Kamala the Saturday before Christmas. D'Ondre had resisted, but Kamala argued that Kennedy, of all people, would have wanted her to come out after a respectful period and if not embrace a social life, at least not turn away from it. "Especially," she said, "not to give up on Christmas."

***

"Welcome, Dee!" Kamala greeted her enthusiastically at the door. She noted, as she took

D'Ondre's coat that she had dressed conservatively, but at least not in black. "Merry Christmas!" she added, determined not to press the issue of Christmas avoidance, but not to avoid it herself, either. It was time for normalization. "Same to you, Kam," D'Ondre replied, and with a genuine smile.

Normalization continued as D'Ondre made her way around, first with Kamala introducing her to people she didn't know, and then greeting mutual friends, some of whom she hadn't seen for a while. A squeeze of a hand, here, and an understanding compressing of lips, there, were sufficiently ambiguous to be interpreted as supportive, without seeming solicitous. One of the introductions was to a good-looking colleague of Kamala's named William. Kamala didn't linger over the introduction past presenting D'Ondre as a very dear, long-time friend and William as a musician and aspiring conductor.

After getting a drink, D'Ondre continued to circulate on her own, catching up with old friends and making new acquaintances keen to find out more about her. At last, there was a break and an opportunity to visit the ladies room and to grab another drink. She walked from the kitchen/dining room bar over to a love seat in the living room, gratified to be able to sit for a bit.

"Is that seat taken?" slid smoothly through William's broad smile. It wasn't a brilliant conversation starter, but the smile was impossible to resist.

"No, it isn't," D'Ondre returned, reflecting his smile.

"Kamala tells me you're an engineer. Well, since I'm a conductor, we already have something in common."

It took D'Ondre a second to get the pun. She raised her eyes, wrinkling her forehead but maintained her smile. "I suppose your next line is that we could make beautiful music together."

The rest seemed to be fate. They were married six months later. William agreed to D'Ondre's request for a simple ceremony and simple gold rings, as well as her desire to move Kennedy's ring to her middle finger. He understood her explanation that she would forever love Kennedy, as the ring signified, in the same way their rings also promised forever love. It was a bit like sharing Kennedy's legacy, but William was self-assured and shrugged it off.

D'Ondre also had suggested that they live in her house. She had had to resist the strong urge within her to start completely over with Wiliam in a new place. She did, however, truly love her house and the trees, and she had convinced herself that the best way to deal with the past was to embrace the good parts and not run away from the bad. For his part, William was fine with becoming the new man of the house. When D'Ondre shared her plans to add on and eventually start a family, he insisted that he would pay for the addition and do "everything I can" to start a family when she was ready.

When their first Christmas came, D'Ondre yielded to his gentle suggestion that they should get a tree and decorate it. To help her make it more completely their own, he took D'Ondre to a cut-your-own tree farm, and they spent a happy afternoon picking out just the right one. When they were preparing to trim it, he tactfully asked D'Ondre if there were any special ornaments Kennedy had brought to their previous trees or had given to her.

D'Ondre probably would have mentioned anyway the ornaments Kennedy had made as a child and the one he had given her on each of their almost two Christmases together. William's bringing it up himself, however, endeared him further to her and created an almost family connection between William, Kennedy, and her. That Christmas was sweet for her and allowed her to embrace the holiday season once again.

The next year flew by, but D'Ondre and William managed to plan out and add two more bedrooms, a master bath, and a living room across the back of the house. Much of one side of the big tree in the back now hung over one of the bedrooms. This caused the builder some concern about falling branches, but they had a tree-trimmer cut back the branches most likely to fall, before construction began. They got the painting and papering done and the new furniture moved in before the really cold weather and were ready just in time for the Christmas holiday season.

It was D'Ondre, this time, who enthused about going back to the same tree farm to cut another perfect tree. They set up the tree and decorated it lovingly, in time for William to fly back home to spend a few days with his parents and return on Christmas Day when "nobody flew."

D'Ondre confirmed that William's return flight was on schedule before leaving for the airport Christmas morning. She got there with plenty of time and parked in the short-term lot. She went in, checked the arrivals screen, and sat in the arrival area to wait. When the posted arrival time had come and gone, she checked again every ten minutes, but the time hadn't changed. The fourth time she checked, the screen changed as she looked as it to "See agent," and she knew. She knew something terrible had happened.

After William's death, D'Ondre swore off Christmas entirely. She wasn't particularly superstitious, but losing two husbands at Christmas made reliving the season really too much to bear. For the next two years, D'Ondre took her vacation time during the Christmas season and in warm places where she could isolate herself as much as possible from everyone else's happy celebration. After the second Christmas, she decided this arrangement had outlived its usefulness and was actually causing her to immerse herself in thinking about what had happened.

When she got back to work, she found that the firm had hired a new engineer named Xavier, with whom she found herself working closely on several projects that year. She came to think of him as "X-man," and after a while started feeling comfortable enough to call him that to his face. They worked together well and started going out for a drink or dinner after work occasionally. By the end of the year, they had become close and Xavier asked her to spend Christmas with him.

D'Ondre was at the point, then, where spending "quality" time with him was quite attractive, but *she* set the terms. They would spend the time at *her* house, and there would be no mention of Christmas. Xavier, who especially liked all the hoopla of Christmas and found her no-Christmas condition a little strange, nevertheless accepted it. He knew that D'Ondre was a widow twice over and suspected that there was a tie-in between this and Christmas. He was reluctant to bring it up with her, so he asked Kamala, who had become a mutual friend.

"Oh yes, there's a connection with Christmas," Kamala affirmed. "First, she's scared to death of getting married again. You know, three strikes and all that. Then, both previous husbands died at Christmas. Dee is a very reasonable person, but even if you discount any karma or whatever behind the coincidence, the emotional baggage is too much for her."

Xavier thought about this and being both a man and an engineer, decided that what he was would figure out a fix for this problem. His plan was to decorate his own apartment, persuade D'Ondre to come there for Christmas Eve, and then go to her house for Christmas Day and for however long things developed. It would be like a Christmas vaccination for her and get it back into her blood without any unpleasant side effects.

It took some gentle nudging, and D'Ondre was distinctly uncomfortable at first on Christmas Eve, but Xavier hadn't overdone the decorations and eased her into the spirit of things. His Christmas Day reservation at her house got extended to several days. They worked it out that two rational, science-oriented people like them had no place in their heads or hearts for any Christmas curses. They were married two months later with Kamala as a relieved and joyous maid of honor. It was another simple ceremony and ring, and D'Ondre moved William's ring to her index finger.

By December of the following year, D'Ondre and Xavier had had several heart-to-hearts on deceased husbands and Christmas. These gave D'Ondre the opportunity to talk freely about Kennedy and William, what good people they had been, and how much she missed them. None of this bothered Xavier at all, and told her, "Dee, I am so happy that you have such a huge capacity for love. It's an honor for me to be in your heart with those other two and on your finger alongside their rings. This is going to last a long, long time."

When Xavier looked for statistical proof that fewer people probably died over the Christmas holiday, though, he was shocked to find that significantly *more* people did die between Christmas and New Year Day than at any other time of the year, with Christmas being the absolute worse single day. He made no attempt to hide the statistics from D'Ondre and found, as he expected, that figuring out reasons for this, such as depression and loneliness, actually made the deadliness of the day more abstract and less ominous.

The high-ceilinged family room that D'Ondre and William had added on and which they both hoped would someday soon be filled with bright-eyed children eager to open presents, was the venue for the shapely, tall tree they had picked out. Tonight was the night for decorating, and with their combination of ornaments, they had done an all-out job. Xavier had

had to use a six-foot step ladder to hang the highest ornaments, and now he was ready for the piece-de-resistance, the tree topper. They had agreed on a multi-colored wreath with its own light that had an open anchor tube at its base to slip onto the top stem of the tree.

Xavier set up the ladder as close as he could to the tree, but with the full tree they had chosen, it was still a reach to get the wreath anchored. On the fourth step, he couldn't quite get it and wished the heck they had an eight-foot ladder. He stepped up one more step, reached, and leaned a little bit too far. He felt himself start to fall into the tree and pushed his shins against the top of the ladder hard and threw his weight back. It was too much, and he started to fall back away from the tree.

Xavier tossed the wreath into the tree with a flick of his wrist and tried to run backwards down the steps of the ladder as fast as he could. His feet flew to the second step and then he had to hop off the remaining distance. When his feet hit the floor, he backpedaled for all he was worth, twirling his arms to right himself. He couldn't regain his balance, however, and he fell backwards and hit his head violently on the corner of a heavy coffee table.

D'Ondre screamed and a wave of mixed horror and despair swept over her. She rushed to Xavier, pressing 911 on her phone at the same time. An ambulance got there within minutes, and the hospital was close by, but Xavier had broken his skull and suffered massive brain injury. He died two days later.

***

D'Ondre took a month-long leave from work to try to come to grips with what was happening to her. A national T.V. news magazine show contacted her about doing a story on her bad luck, but she angrily shut its reporter down. Even had she not found it cruelly exploitative, she herself didn't know what to think or what to do about her freakish distinction. By the end of a month, she had worked through the facts of it. It would take much longer, she knew, to overcome her grief.

Reasonable person that she was and honoring the discussions she had had with Xavier, she knew she couldn't believe there was any occult power or wrinkle in the texture of the universe that was targeting her. The tie between Christmas and her husbands' deaths had to be coincidence. Regardless, simple logic told her that it couldn't happen again if she never had another husband. She vowed this time to never marry again. She wouldn't try to avoid Christmas, but she also knew that she would never be able to embrace it because of what it represented for her.

Life went on for D'Ondre. It was almost easier this time because it almost seemed normal to have a husband who had died. There definitely was a void, however, and she filled it, in part, by throwing herself into her work. Because she was good at what she did, this paid off in conventional ways. She thought of the irony of Kennedy's wanting to work hard to impress his boss and achieve success. "Success isn't all it's cracked up to be," she thought. "It doesn't fill the empty spot where husband and children should go."

Outside of work, D'Ondre immersed herself in reading. She also tried social media for a while, but she found it made her feel very lonely. She concluded that if she really were lonely, finding friends in books was probably more substantial than finding them online. This was more prophetic than she might have imagined. She joined a book club through the library, without even a thought to finding new friends but because she genuinely wanted to discuss books.

This worked out well, and she grew even more enthusiastic about both the intellectual and the social aspects of meeting around and discussing books. She decided that a book club organized around her professional interests might also be good, and she discovered and joined a second through a local engineering society. This also worked well for her. She found a mutuality of mind but one that was based on a respect for facts, reason, and their application. There were, however, a host of different facts and applications to consider, which occasionally led to some rather heated discussions, as well as a definite tendency to reading science fiction. It turned out to be both intellectual stimulus and genuine fun at the same time.

When Aman was invited to join the engineering book club, D'Ondre found him particularly interesting because he was a Buddhist. This led to a quite different perspective on the books they read. After a few months, she and Aman started continuing club discussions over tea at a nearby teahouse. Before long, the discussion of books included personal philosophies to support opinions, and then their personal lives.

When the subject of karma came up in Aman's describing Buddhism, it caused D'Ondre a considerable amount of thought and not a little consternation. As she and Aman got to know each other better, she felt a need to tell him about the Christmas curse. This was partly because they had grown much closer but even more because she really wanted to see how karma might apply to it. She liked the justice aspect of karma, but she couldn't subscribe to the reality of a non-physical cosmic force behind it. Nevertheless, she had a little itch of curiosity that needed scratching over some sort of responsibility she might bear.

After she had told Aman about Kennedy, William, and Xavier, she waited for him to respond without influencing his response. He looked at her with pain on his own face. "Oh, D'Ondre, that is such a heavy burden for you to have to carry, and not just once but three times over. I wish there had been something through all that I could have done to ease your pain."

D'Ondre edged towards what she really wanted to ask him. "Thank you, Aman. I think if I had known you along the way, you probably could have helped. What you've told me already about acceptance and mindfulness and letting beauty in surely would have been helpful, and it is right now. I really want to explore these further with you, but there's something else that I want to ask you.

"When you talked about karma, it made me think. Under that idea, could it be that something I did could have influenced my husbands' fate? I mean, three times the same circumstances. Honestly, I've thought this through thoroughly, and I've accepted what happened intellectually--and I don't feel guilty. Still, I'm curious to know what karma might say about my role in it."

Aman immediately knew his answer; nevertheless, he chose his words carefully. His nature was to respond with loving kindness, but beyond that, his feelings for D'Ondre had developed into more than those for a mere discussion partner. "What I think is if you feel any sort of responsibility, it should only be to learn from what's happened and become an even more enlightened person than you already are.

"Look, I know already that you are a beautiful soul. I know that your karma is good, but what you do doesn't necessarily apply. The justice part of karma comes from the *intention* behind the actions much more than the actions themselves. Plus, the consequences aren't immediate, and they don't apply individually. The entire body applies in your next life. I'm thinking that means something good for you next time around and probably for at least one other individual, then."

It was the right things to say. It was the right things to convince D'Ondre that Aman must have done some pretty good things in his own previous life and that she likely was the other individual to benefit from that. She was ready to find out.

***

D'Ondre and Aman grew together and grew ever closer together. Christmas Eve afternoon that year found them cuddling quietly on the couch in the sitting room at the front of D'Ondre's house. They could see inky clouds approaching from the west that promised a serious snowstorm, which made hunkering down even more attractive.

"I think I'll check the weather to see what we're in for," D'Ondre said and got up to find the remote to turn on the TV. "It's almost time for the weather report. "

Sure enough, they were right in the path of a major storm, and one with a twist. "If you're in the path of this storm, you might get to see a pretty rare phenomenon," said the announcer. "There's already been reports of lightning associated with this storm. You may get to experience thundersnow."

"Wow!" D'Ondre said, "Wouldn't that be something." She turned off the TV and came back to the couch the same time as Aman who had gotten up to fetch something from his coat. "Did you hear that?"

"Mmm," he acknowledged as they both sat down. "D'Ondre," he continued, "I'm not exactly a man of a few words, so I'm going to make you a simple proposition in a somewhat un-simple way. You know I've come to love you deeply. I've also come to think it's fate that's brought us together." He smiled playfully at this last. "What I know is I want to spend the rest of my life with you—and any future one's, for that matter." Smile again.

"I also know you've sworn off marriage and wedding rings, and I fully understand why. I think that's no barrier to two people's marrying their lives together, to planning and expecting they will love each other and make each other as happy as they can, for as long as they can. I don't think any ceremony, any document, or anyone's sanction is necessary to bring this sacred trust about. In modern parlance, I'm asking, "Will you be my forever partner in love?" I'm doing this on Christmas Eve in the name of Kennedy, William, and Xavier, to erase all the pain and sorrow for you associated with what should be a time of joy, and make it from this day forward just that, a time of new and lasting joy."

D'Ondre was stunned. She had no idea this was coming. The shock, instead of rendering her numb and incapable of thinking what to do, jump started both her brain and her emotions and made it unnecessary for Aman to even think about saying, "If you need some time to think about it . . ." Like three cherries on a slot machine, the words came up on her lips, "Oh Aman, yes."

After a long, loving embrace, Aman said, "That takes care of marriage. To replace *wedding* rings:" he produced two small boxes, each with two exquisitely filigreed gold dharmachakra wheels* set up as earrings. After explaining their symbolism, he said, "I figured we'd skip ring number four and go right to five gold rings. And you won't have to wear a ring on your pinky finger. Two are for you. The other two are for me. I believe it has become quite fashionable for men to wear gold earrings," he quipped.

D'Ondre was stunned at his thoughtfulness and kissed him deeply. At the same time, there was a flash of lightning, an enormous blast of thunder, and an explosion that rattled the windows. D'Ondre clung tightly to Aman, her mind frozen in terror in automatic response to the assumed disaster to follow.

What followed immediately was a loud RIIIIIIIIP, a lusty SWOOOOSH, and a mighty CRASH! The crash brought her back to reality, and she cried, "The tree, oh my god, the tree."

She and Aman rushed to the front door, tore it open, and there was half of the huge willow oak lying across the snow in the front yard, away from the house.

***

D'Ondre and Aman waited inside for a half hour before feeling it was safe to venture out to look at the tree, which *could have* come down on top of the house with disastrous results.

"Aman, you can be sure I don't believe in "signs," but if there ever was a sign, this is it. The curse is broken, and you are safe."

When they were back inside, D'Ondre said with an impish look on her face that hadn't been there for a long time. "You know what I think we're going to do? There's a tree lot on Oak St. that looked as if it still had some trees left this morning. I think we're going to go get us a tree and put it up in the family room. We aren't going to decorate it because I don't have any decorations. What we're going to do is put a blanket down in front of it and see what we can do to make some kids to fill these bedrooms."

Aman agreed immediately.

*The dharmachakra is a Buddhist emblem of Hindu origin. It resembles a wagon wheel with eight spokes, each representing one of the eight tenets of

Buddhist belief. Each spoke is said to have sharp edges to cut through ignorance. The circle symbolizes the perfection of the dharma; the hub stands for discipline, which is the core of meditation practice; the rim refers to the mindfulness or samadhi which holds everything together and the spokes represent the eightfold path leading to enlightenment:

Right faith, right intention, right speech, right action, right livelihood, right endeavor, right mindfulness, and right meditation.

It is drawn from an Indian symbol which represents samsara, or endless rebirth. But to Buddhists it symbolizes overcoming obstacles. The dharma wheel can also refer to the dissemination of the dharma from country to country. In this sense the dharma wheel began rolling in India, carried on to Central Asia, arrived in South East and East Asia and ultimately the West and the world.

Mark Defrates Jewelry,
http://www.markdefrates.com/pages/buddhist.html

City Lights for Christmas

Jesus Roberto Bengochea was excited, which was nothing new, as anyone who lived on his street could tell you. He was also on a mission, another of his well-known characteristics. This mission was so new the ink was still wet where he signed on to it, hence the excitement. He walked fast, with purpose towards Alden St. from the closest bus stop on Washington Ave. where the afternoon bus still stopped.

J.R., as he preferred to be called, regularly came up with ideas and projects to go with them. Mrs. Hatcher next door told him she thought he'd be mayor someday and get the city out of its shameful bankruptcy. "You got ideas, J.R.," she said, "and you're not afraid of work, either." It was a new idea that was moving him now, and he was ready to go to work on it, though he had no idea of how to do it or what it would involve

His family was relatively new to the neighborhood, having only moved in five years ago. His papa got a new job at a close-by auto plant when GM shut down the one where he had been working. His parents chose not to move to Mexicantown on the other side of the big city, even though the area was much nicer, and houses there were cheaper than day-old tortillas. His father thereby avoided the long and tedious drive across town.

The downside was that houses were cheap because people were mostly moving out of this part of the city. Many of the houses on Alden Street had gone vacant, foreclosed on, or just abandoned as people lost jobs. Seniority, a specialized skill, and another worker's fortunate retirement made his father one of the lucky ones in a down economy. To J.R., who loved his street and his neighbors, the exodus from the city was a crying shame. But he saw it also as a great opportunity, as it had been for his family. The people left on his street were good neighbors and committed to the neighborhood. The houses, an eclectic mix of bungalows, foursquares, and Cape Cods were thoroughly middle class, except for the house at the end of his cul-de-sac street, the one his neighbors called "The mansion" or, sometimes, "The haunted house." It was this house that was the source of J.R.'s current excitement.

He was coming from the dusty archives of the main branch of the public library, where he had been researching the history of his neighborhood, and Alden Street in particular. As a homeschooler, he was at the library frequently and had become an excellent researcher. He discovered that the street's namesake, Henry Alden, was one of the first inventors made well off by the auto industry. When he hit it big, Alden bought the land for Alden St. and developed the street as a neighborhood of modest homes, anchored by his own grand Queen Ann at the end—the mansion.

The 2½ story Alden House had double high peaked gables for front second story windows bisected on top by a third gable for the "attic" windows. Wide steps rose to the middle of the broad, conversation porch, outlined with rails with round carved spindles. The porch was covered with a red-tiled canopy to match the main roof and supported by four columns with plain round shafts. The center entrance had its own small gable to match those above. The house itself, a faded slate blue with cream trim, fairly begged to become a painted lady. It was hardly a mansion but was, nevertheless impressive compared to its neighbors.

J.R. had found a 1935 newspaper article with a picture of the Alden house aglow with Christmas lights outlining every line and angle, and he was determined to make that happen again. The accompanying article related how Alden wanted to bring some Christmas cheer to a neighborhood awash with the Great Depression. J.R. was immediately struck by the comparisons to the more recent Great

Recession and its aftermath and the need for a similar uplift for the survivors on Alden Street. His mission was to light up the abandoned mansion on Alden St. once again for Christmas.

"It's going to be so cool," he was thinking as he walked, "to get the mansion lit up for Christmas again. But how we gonna do it?" he said out loud. "So many people on the street looking for work or maybe losing their house." This was only a fleeting check on his enthusiasm, and he pushed it to the back of his mind. His plan, for now, was that he *was* going to do it; *how* would take care of itself, and his pace quickened.

He sprinted up the concrete steps to his front porch as if his idea or his enthusiasm or both would expire if he didn't share them with someone soon. He pulled open the heavy oak front door with a shower of tingling bells, somewhat careful, at least, not to disturb his mother's elaborate decorations covering its three-quarter glass light. "Mama, I have the greatest idea!"

"It is a beautiful idea, Jesus," his mother agreed when he had blurted out what he wanted to do. "*Muy Bueno*. It will be a specially beautiful present for both baby Jesus and for you on your birthday."

J.R. almost forgot in his excitement that Christmas was his own birthday—almost, but not quite. It was pretty hard to forget when he had been challenged or teased all his life by Anglos who thought it was either weird or sacrilegious to be named "Jesus." It didn't help at all to explain that it was because he was born on December 25th. There had even been one mythical prodigy who had come up with the bright idea of calling him "Hey, Zeus!" All of this made the switch to "J.R." a practical necessity.

"But how you gonna do it, *mi carino*? First, you have to get permission from whoever owns that place. Then you have to get a lot of lights somewhere. Then you have to put them up on the house somehow. That's a whole lot of *obstaculos*. The people on this street are good neighbors, and I'm sure they would help, but they are not so wealthy, you know."

"I know, I know, Mamma, but this is so right, it's gotta works. It is going to work."

***

"Well, Mr. Bengochea, it looks like you're in luck—or not." J.R.'s father had been right when he advised him to start looking for the Alden house owners at City Hall. Both the City Clerk, Betty Harris, and the tax assessor she called in for consultation had warmed up to J.R.'s enthusiasm and story, and it hadn't taken them long to find what he was looking for. "The City has foreclosed on this as abandoned property and now owns it, so if you want to do anything to it, you'll have to get permission from the city. "And," Ms. Harris continued, "I'm sure that anyone actively participating in any such project would have to be insured. It's a fine idea you have, J.R., but…"

"It's still a fine idea," J.R. replied. Two hours later, having charmed Ms. Harris into exceptional customer service, they listened to a city attorney who determined that the city would be legally responsible. "But, that means," the attorney told him, just as Ms.

Harris had predicted, "that whoever does the installing will have to have liability insurance, as well." Then, the clerk helped him get the permit forms to be signed.

"Thank you so much," J.R. told Ms. Harris as they left the attorney's office. "I hope you will come to Alden St. to see the lights you helped get up."

"Well, I'm afraid that now you need to find someone to put those light up, but, you know, I'll bet you can do it, and I *will* come by to see them. Good luck, J.R. Say, what does "J.R." stand for?"

When J.R. told her and explained the circumstances behind his first name, she said, "Well then, I *am* betting on you. It looks like you might have friends in high places."

***

"Before I get someone to put the lights up," J.R. thought after saying goodbye to Ms. Harris, "I gotta get some lights, lots of lights." Later, his father told him their family could kick in $50 towards buying lights, but with Christmas looming and his brothers and sisters to buy gifts for, that was already stretching it.

"You can put in whatever you would spend on me," J.R. offered.

"Where do you think that $50 is coming from," his father laughed.

That afternoon and evening, he visited up and down Alden St. explaining what he wanted to do and soliciting help. With all the empty houses, it didn't take long.

Mrs. Hatcher said that her Social Security check just barely let her scrape by. If she didn't have her house paid off, she would have been gone a long time ago, too.

Reverend Bullock told him that his small congregation is contributing everything they can to help out families even less fortunate than they are.

The Johnsons started off with saying they were more into Kwanzaa than Christmas, but J.R. surprised them with his knowledge of such by saying that most of the principles of Kwanzaa have to do with community, and the lighting of candles could be symbolized through the lighting of the lights on the "community mansion." He came away with $20.

Mrs. Bernstein, who was reputed to have lived on Alden St. forever, asked him if he understood what Hanukkah is, to which he replied, "The Festival of Lights, Mrs. Bernstein. It's perfect! We will make this our festival of the lights." Impressed, she told him that as a child she had known Henry Alden. "He was a very enlightened man. This street was always a neighborhood of great diversity, and the people appreciated that. He loved Christmas, and Christian or not, every house on this street used to be lit up with Christmas lights." She thanked J.R. for what he was trying to do and gave him $20.

He used this story and similar logic on Jessie Jones, a young man with a new family who was trying to get through a community college program to start a career. Jones said that he wasn't a believer, but J.R. said it didn't matter. "We got us a very diverse community here. So what if we're not all Christian. Christmas means a lot more than religious stuff. I read the other day that the early Christians borrowed Christmas from the pagans! It's the Christmas spirit that counts. We all got that."

Jones was moved by J.R.'s speech, but he said he still was up against a wall financially and couldn't spare a cent. He did, however, say he would be glad to help with whatever work on the project that was needed.

By the time he was done, J.R. had $150 and a several promises of help putting up the lights. As he went to sleep that night, he was puzzling over how he was going to get the rest of the money for the lights and how he was going to get the darned things up.

J.R.'s sleep was troubled by ongoing dreams of stringing lights at the mansion. Mrs. Hatcher kept apologizing for not contributing to the lights fund and saying she wanted to *string them* anyway. Jesse Jones and Jennifer O'Neal from up the street came into the picture, each on one end of a long, long ladder. Mrs. Hatcher said over and over, "It's about time you got here," as a bunch of anonymous hands raised the ladder to the side of the house. Mrs. Hatcher jumped onto the ladder and shouted, "Give me lights!" and Mrs. Bernstein was busy taking bulbs out of a large basket and screwing them into sockets as the Mrs. Hatcher pulled the string up.

Mrs. Bernstein gave J.R. a dirty look each time she plucked another bulb, and Mrs. Hatcher yelled down, "I'll bet these bulbs are the kind if one burns out they all go out." J.R. kept saying very defensively, "I'm *sorry*, it was the best I could do. All we could afford are these old lights left over from fifty years ago."

J.R.'s eyes opened and he was suddenly awake. "That's it!" he said aloud. "There has to be some left over lights somewhere. There must be something like a new model every year, like GM does with its cars, or at least every once in a while. Somebody's got some leftovers stashed in a warehouse somewhere."

Back at the library the next day, a librarian helped him research surplus Christmas lights. Unfortunately, he was unable to discover anything that was close to being discounted enough to stretch $150 to cover the number of lights he figured they would need.

Discouraged after an hour or so of fruitless searching the Internet and phone books, he went back to the library research desk and asked the librarian if she had any other ideas. She thought about it for a bit and said, "With the city's financial problems, we librarians are acutely aware of cutbacks. We haven't been able to buy books, except from money earned from used book sales. I don't suppose there are any used Christmas light sales, but the city does have a big warehouse of surplus property." Thinking out loud, she continued, "But, I can't imagine they'd have used lights for sale.

"Wait, the city always strings miles of lights downtown. I'll bet they're cutting back on that, too, this year. They probably have leftovers. They might be willing to sell off some of their lights, or even let you use some, if you know the right person to ask."

***

When J.R. showed up at Betty Harris's office again, it wasn't much of a surprise. The combination of his determination and the problematic nature of his project had made it likely. Betty Harris smiled at him and asked, "How can I help you, J.R?

J.R. smiled back; it was the right question to ask. "Well, Ms. Harris, I don't know if you can, but I sure appreciate you asking. You always seem to know the right people to call, and that's what I need right now." He unfolded his thinking that since the city owned the Alden house, and since the city probably had lots of spare Christmas lights, and since the city probably wanted to let people know it was still a great place to live, and since it *was* Christmas time...

"I think I see where you're going with this, J.R., and it's crazy, but I suppose not any more crazy than this whole thing you're trying to do. And it *is* Christmas time..." she trailed off, herself, into thought for a few moments. "I'm the City Clerk, not a miracle worker, but let me see what I can do. Call me later this afternoon."

When J.R. called, Ms. Harris told him that his luck was holding, and his story continued to work its magic. "The Parks Department hasn't hung light for several years. It's all done by private sponsors now, so there are miles of lights ready and waiting for you to use. By "you," though, I mean you have to find someone who's bonded and insured to do that sort of thing. I don't guess I can help you there. I asked, but Parks & Rec has definitely reached its limit with letting you use some lights."

"Thank you, Ms. Harris. You are *such* a big help. I'll figure it out some way."

Betty Harris nodded an appreciative agreement as he left. "And I'll bet you will."

***

J.R. kept going back to his dream about Mrs. Hatcher on the long ladder. In his dream, she was all the way up to the central dormer atop the third story roof. He chuckled as he pictured old Mrs. Hatcher so high up. When he thought of it, he realized how much of an angle the ladder would need to be pitched to get over the canopy roof across the deep front porch to put up lights up on the front dormer. "That's just scary," he realized with a shiver. "I sure wouldn't want to be stretched out off something like that trying to string lights. Man, what we need is one of those cherry pickers things."

Just then, he heard the blare and bells of a fire engine, probably on Washington Ave., and a solution sprung into his head. The city, financially strapped as it was, had come through for him so far. Why not one more time?

When J. R. laid out the whole project to the captain at the fire station closest to his house, the fire fighter laughed ironically and said, "We're lucky that this station hasn't been closed. The department staff has been cut, and we can't always respond to calls in a timely manner or at all. And you want us to hang Christmas lights?"

J.R. kept quiet. He was learning that the best way to get people to help is to let them talk themselves into it.

"Did you know that half of the fires these days are arson? Probably some young punks having fun. Hey, let's burn down this vacant house. Who cares? And you want us to dress up an abandoned place?

"You know, that's actually refreshing, a young guy like you coming up with that. You say it's a city-owned house and Parks are supplying the lights? Black Friday, the day after Thanksgiving is usually pretty slow, with everybody out shopping. Let me do some checking, and I'll see what we can do.

**

"Papa, look what I've done," J.R. greeted his father proudly when he came home from work. His father, used to making car parts that had to fit precisely with the whole, listened patiently as his son explained how everything was going to work. J.R. finished with: "Maybe someone will see the mansion and want to buy it, and maybe that would start people moving back onto Alden St.!"

"*Bien heco*" his father said, but with a hint of skepticism. He raised his forehead and tilted his head. "And where are you going to plug in these lights?"

J.R.'s triumph made a U turn to consternation, but only briefly. He had come too far on this project to let a small thing like its not being plugged in stop him or ruin his good mood. Pointing to the electrical outlet near the front door, he came back with, "We can get a long extension cord and plug it in here, Papa"

His father lowered his eyebrows then raised them as he got the joke. "And, how are we going to pay for this power?"

"I have one hundred and fifty dollars!"

"That might be enough just to get the power turned back on at the Alden house," his father said, shaking his head ironically, "but those lights will use *mucho* electricity."

The reality of the situation finally caught up with J.R.. For the first time since the start of this whole odyssey, his bravado failed him with the finish line being pulled away just as he was about to cross it.

"Don't worry, *socio*. With your *audacia*, your mama's practicality, and my engineering, we can surely work this one out. "If we share ideas, we can come up with a solution."

J.R. had felt pretty good going it alone so far, but now he felt a surge of relief that his parents were going to help.

As they all sat at the kitchen table, his father asked him to review again what he had done so far and where the project stood. After J.R. had gone over it, his mother summed it up. "It looks like you keep going with the city, and the city is going with you. That's a really good *colaboracion*, but the city doesn't own an electric company."

"Ah but the electric company does, his father offered. And I've heard that the electric company is sponsoring the downtown Christmas tree and all of its thousands of lights. Your project would be *tarea facil* for them, don't you think, Jesus?" J.R.'s countenance brightened, and he nodded his head thoughtfully.

The next day, J.R. started with the tried and true. Ms. Harris steered him to the person at Parks in charge of the Christmas decorations in the downtown plaza. She, in turn, called a contact she had at the power company, who put her through to the P.R. officer, who said he would be glad to talk with J.R. J.R. worked his magic once more, and the string of circumstances was complete and plugged in to power that would be checked, turned on, and supplied by City Edison.

The magic of this cooperation went farther, however, as each section, separately and then together, realized the public relations value of what they were doing. Contacts were made among them for a smoother operation. Others were activated so that overnight a full-blown campaign was born that would let the world know what one precocious *muchacho* was doing to try to revitalize his street and his city when the lights went on. J.R.'s intentions had been quite a bit more modest, but he was more than willing to embrace this wider scope of idealism and the potential of celebrity it involved.

The last occurred to him when the daily newspaper arranged an interview with him for the major story they'd be doing on lighting up the Alden house and "the city's dark times" as part of a Christmas in the City series. Everything was turning out better than J.R. could have ever imagined.

***

The week before Thanksgiving, J.R. got a call from Betty Harris. "You don't know how much I hate to tell you this J.R. You've worked so hard on lighting up the holidays for a lot of people. But I have someone who has put a bid on the house and wants to seal the deal right away. If the city no longer owns the house, the lights, putting them up, and I'm pretty sure the power are all not going to happen. I'm really, really sorry, J.R."

J.R. was stunned. This was a snowball rolling downhill that hits a tree square on at the bottom and explodes. His brain, drowning for a moment in despair, began reaching for some sort of lifeline. "Ms. Harris, can't we talk this guy out of buying the house?"

"Oh J.R., you know that's what we all would like to do, but the city's interest in the house is to sell it and get the money to compensate it for the unpaid taxes. It's our job."

"Well, what if we outbid him and bought the house?"

"Even if you could somehow raise the money, you would own the house and not the city, so you'd have to come up with even more money for the lights. And there isn't time, J.R.; this man has made all the arrangements, including having a check in hand for the purchase price."

"Maybe we can ask him to wait until after the holidays; then, we can still do it."

"I told him about you and the lights, and he said he knew about you and he wasn't interested in waiting."

"I been thinking about how these lights might make the house worth more and interest someone in buying it. He could make some money on it if it's famous. We should tell him that."

"Actually, J.R., I kind of brought that up, but I think he wants to tear the house down, so he doesn't want the price to go up."

"Oh Ms. Harris, there's got to be *something* I can do."

"Well J.R., you could try doing what you've been doing right along with this. *You* could try talking to him. I have his contact information. But, to be fair, I don't think there's much of a chance. You shouldn't get your hopes up for this, but you *can* try."

***

J.R. was quite surprised when Scott Woods not only agreed to talk with him but had suggested coming to the city, a big relief for J.R. since he didn't know how he would have been able to meet Woods at his office thirty some miles away. Woods had also suggested they meet at a deli on Washington Avenue and told J.R. he'd buy him lunch. Woods had been very businesslike in his manner. Combined with his willingness to meet, this left J.R. puzzled about what the outcome might be. Did Mr. Woods feel sorry for him and just want to smooth things out?

He got to the Star Deli fifteen minute early and got a booth in the back where it would be the most quiet in the noisy restaurant. He told the cashier he was expecting Mr. Woods and asked him to direct him to the right place. J.R. fidgeted and played with the salt and pepper shakers, but he didn't have long to wait. In five minutes, a thirty-something man wearing a plaid wool jacket and blue jeans greeted him.

"Hello J.R. I'm glad to meet you. I was waiting for you to call, and you didn't disappoint me." J.R. was stunned at this revelation. Woods took off his jacket, laid it on the seat, and sat down. "So, tell me about your interest in this house."

This put the shoe on the other foot for J.R., who expected to listen and respond to Woods's interest in the house. But he was entirely comfortable with his own narrative and went on, interrupted only by the waitperson taking their order and a few requests for clarification from Woods.

When their food came, Woods encouraged J.R. to dig in, but J.R. was deeply and passionately into his story of his research into Henry Alden, his plan to light up the house as it was in the old days, his arrangements with the city, and his plea that if Mr. Woods could only wait to close his deal until after New Year's, it would make him a hero.

Finally, he got it all out and was glad to start in on his sandwich and fries and let Woods talk.

"That's all very interesting, J.R. I actually knew most of that. I have a good friend who is a writer for the newspaper, and he filled me in on most of it. It actually plays a big part in why I decided to buy the Alden house."

This did not sound good to J.R. *His plan* was actually a reason why Mr. Woods bought the house? He had actually been working *against* himself? His food, once again, didn't seem very interesting.

"Let me explain. I'm a carpenter and a builder. I've actually had my eye on the Alden house for a while. I think the city might be ready to turn a corner and make a comeback. I think there are better neighborhoods, for sure, that will lead the way, but I also think there are pockets here and there that could be what you might call seeds for *run-down* neighborhoods to grow back. Those really interest me because that's where properties are very cheap. The trick is picking the right neighborhoods, the right streets, and the right houses."

This all sounded good and right to J.R. It was a more explicit version of what he had been thinking all along.

"So, you've got Alden Street, a not-too-bad-yet street with substantial houses that are still in good shape. And, or maybe I should say "but," you have the big house, unlike the others, that anchors the street. Maybe it's restorable and maybe it's not, but would someone want to live in a house unlike all the others on the street?"

This was now seeming to J.R. more and more like an explanation of why the house should be torn down, and his spirits were sinking like the mouthful of sandwich he had just swallowed.

"Here's the thing. I want to be sure that this street has the grit and determination to make a comeback. That's why your efforts were so interesting and why I wanted to meet you to see if you were for real. Your description of your neighbors has also been a confirmation for me that this is a deal I should go through with.

"Now, I know you have a keen interest in what I'm going to do with the Alden house. It's like this, J.R.; the house could be torn down and a new one, maybe two, put up eventually that went with the rest of the street, because, as I said before, 'Who would want to live in the big house?'"

"The fact is, I have been considering living there myself. I believe in this city, and I think the house is very livable and with a workable investment could be restored to its former grandness. I think you would make a fine neighbor, along with the other people on the street. And, I myself have deep roots in this street and this house. You see, my great uncle was Henry Alden."

***

Scott Woods deferred his deal with the city until after the lighting of Alden House. It turned out that he was also going to buy six other vacant houses on the street for almost nothing. The publicity generated by the newspaper spread, a local T.V. story that made the national news, and the mansion's being voted one of the city's best decorated houses created a good deal of interest in the neighborhood. Scott Woods made out well on his six houses. The other vacant houses got residents, and Alden St. became a key part of the city's renaissance.

Jesus Benochea earned an associate degree in construction from the local community college and is working as an apprentice for Woods, helping to flip houses.

Philosophy of Christmas

Lucy Zhang took a sip from her steaming cup of tea, leaned back in her office chair, closed her eyes, and let the stresses of a long semester begin to lift from her mind like a morning fog after days of rain. It had been a good semester, but six classes and the high intellectual expectations she had for her students put extreme demands on her time and attention. This was compounded by the static of community college add-ons-- committee assignments, record keeping, generic meetings, professional development—that interfered with her focus on teaching.

She still had a week of details to cope with to close out the semester before Christmas break, but a week to work on them seemed itself like a vacation. Still, a wisp of loss over not seeing her students every week crept through her meditation. She and her students had grown quite close as they pursued and developed their individual philosophies of life under the rubric of her *Introduction to Philosophy, Critical Thinking,* and *Introduction to Ethics* courses. This reflected Lucy's approach to philosophy courses for community college students. Creating understanding by making the subject matter relevant to students' own lives worked well for her.

A knock on her office door interrupted her brief reverie. She could see it was Tanya Wells from her ethics class, and she waved her to come in.

"Hey, Tanya. What's up?" Lucy asked, with the comfortable informality that characterized her relationship with her students.

"Ms. Z, I have an ethical dilemma."

Lucy was immediately intent, her practitioner's curiosity rising to a challenge. "Okay, Tanya, have a seat, and let's talk about it."

Tanya sat and began. "Well, Ms. Z., it's like this. You know I'm a parent."

"Yes, you brought that up in class, and it led to some good discussions."

"I have two children of my own."

"Matthew and Melinda, if I remember correctly. And a foster child?"

"That's right," and Tanya paused briefly to get her thoughts together, then continued, choosing her words carefully. "Justin, our foster child, is.....well, he's mean sometimes. He does things that seem to be deliberately hurtful sometimes and at least completely inconsiderate at other times."

A quip about the relevance of ethics to everyday life sprung to Lucy's lips, but she repressed it. She could see that Tanya was seriously distressed.

"Yesterday, in a single day, he got called to the principal's office for sassing his teacher and then got detention for getting into a fight over some kind of name calling. Then at dinner, he was teasing Matthew about his speech impediment, and when I told him to stop, he told me to shut up and I wasn't his mother. I try to talk to him, especially in light of what I've been learning in class, but he doesn't want to talk.

"None of this is new; in fact, it got old real fast when the court sent him to us from my cousin three months ago. I know all of this goes along with being a foster parent, and we're all prepared to work with him over a period of time, but here's the problem."

As Tanya paused again, the irony of Tanya's presenting her with a problem struck Lucy. She had been giving her students problems to think about all semester. Being a sort of big sister to her students, many of whom were older than she and most of whom had problems that made being a student difficult, was another extra role she'd had to assume. It was one, however, that she actually enjoyed, despite its being frequently frustrating.

"Christmas is coming up fast, and I just don't know what to do about presents for Justin. The whole premise of Christmas is the naughty and nice thing."

Lucy laughed to herself. She was sure that Tanya would never have used the word "premise" before having taken her "Inro" class.

"You know: "He knows when you've been bad or good," and bad kids get a lump of coal, and all that. It's a matter of justice and just deserts."

"It is indeed." Lucy smiled inside; this was getting good.

"So," Tanya went on, "if I give Justin what he *deserves*, a lump of coal might be generous."

This was posed as speculation, so Lucy asked, "What do you think he ought to get?"

"That's what I'm struggling with. On the surface, and what I immediately feel is that he deserves a good spanking, but I know that's not right. But based on his actions, justice wouldn't be served by rewarding him for bad behavior."

"Are there other considerations, based on deserts" Lucy probed.

Tanya smiled, "Well, I could make him go without dessert for a month."

"Good one," Lucy said, with a chuckle of appreciation. She encouraged humor in her classroom as a learning tool and to lighten up her rather serious subject matter. Tanya's play on words was a good return on her investment.

"But seriously, Professor Zhang, if I go back to some of the values we discussed, I think him being a human being is one, and he deserves something for that. And he hasn't really harmed anyone, he's just . . . I guess "rude" or "inconvenient" are the words. He doesn't conform to social norms and expectations, you know, but his actions can still feel hurtful at times.

"And he's also my cousin's kid, so I feel a kind of family responsibility there; that's why I took him in. I definitely want to do what's right by him; he's had a hard time of it. I don't think he's ever had a good Christmas with my irresponsible cousin. The thing is, the real issue here is, the results. How will he respond to his Christmas present? What is he going to learn from Christmas? Especially, what will he learn about justice?"

"Ah, pragmatic issues," Lucy replied.

"Exactly."

Lucy pondered this for a moment before answering. "You've learned well that the way to find answers is to ask questions. You certainly asked a few in class," she said smiling, 'and that's why you're getting an "A."

It was Tanya's turn to smile.

"In normal circumstances, how do you think presents make a child feel?"

"Well, thinking back to my own experience, I think loved, appreciated. And *valued*. Maybe he needs to be shown he has value. The self-esteem thing."

"Okay. . ."

"But what if he doesn't feel worthy. It's hard to tell if Justin feels *cheated* by the lack of attention from his mother or that he *deserves* the abuse she's given him."

"So, it seems," Lucy said, "if justice is the issue, justice in your eyes and justice in his, you need to come up with a way to accomplish both. Do you have any ideas on how to achieve that?"

Tanya gave a small sigh of frustration. "I really don't. I guess that's why I came here."

"I'll tell you what, Tanya. You're asking the right questions, and that's way more than half of solving a problem. From what I know about you, if you think about it a bit more, I'll bet you come up with a good answer. If you keep in mind what you know about Justin and about human nature and the likely effects of whatever you do, and if you balance these with your own values, I'm sure you'll do the right thing."

"Thank you, Professor Zhang. I don't have any more answers than I did before, but I feel a lot better about finding some."

"Let me know what happens. Happy holidays!"

***

The week before classes started again, Lucy was in her office, looking at her class rosters and planning out the first week of classes. Recharged after two weeks off, she was eager to get back with students again. She smiled as she came across familiar names on her class rosters. As the college's only philosophy instructor, she often had the same students for all her classes. There was a knock on her door, and she looked up to see Tanya Welles.

Lucy waved Tanya in and invited her to sit down. "I'm so glad to see you, Tanya. I'm excited to see how you solved your Christmas present dilemma." She didn't say "If." She'd had Tanya for three classes, and if she knew her as she thought she did, there were no "ifs" about it.

"Before I say anything, Professor Zhang, I have pictures," Tanya said, and she produced a small album with about a dozen prints.

"Okay, this is our tree all decorated up, with present under it for all the kids."

"It's beautiful, Tanya. You do a really fine job of decorating."

"Mmm. There are ornaments from three generations—now four. We care a lot about family, Tanya said, beaming. This is Matthew opening his first present, and this is Melanie."

Lucy saw two obviously excited children in their pajamas.

"Ah," said Lucy, these are even more beautiful. I see happiness, here."

"Ah," Tanya mimicked, "what is happiness?" And they both laughed.

"Now, here's what I really want you to see. This is Justin opening his first present.

Lucy was suddenly sobered by the sullen looking child, so obviously *unhappy*, holding a piece of paper on which Lucy could discern "Read Me First!" She looked up at Tanya quizzically.

Tanya was still smiling. "But look at these later ones," and she turned to other pictures of Justin looking surprised, then another opening a box, awash with wrapping paper, and *smiling*.

"Okay, my prized student," Lucy said with mock seriousness. "Explain. Evidently you solved your dilemma?"

"It pretty much solved itself," Tanya answered. "Of course, it started with your class."

"Of course," Lucy echoed cheerily.

"Then, with Christmas coming on, I heard that song "Santa Claus Is Coming to Town," and I kept thinking about that line, "He knows if you've been bad or good, so be good for goodness sake." I really didn't think Justin would ever be good for goodness sake. And I thought about the implied threat of the song and the whole justice issue. You know that was going nowhere."

"And you worked it out how?" Lucy asked, eager to hear how what seemed to be a happy ending got that way.

"Weeel . . . I had a little help from Santa. I assumed Santa knew all about pay it forward, like you mentioned in class, and I asked him to write Justin a letter. That's what he's starting to look at in that first picture."

"The letter says that Santa knows you haven't been as good as you could be, Justin. Santa says he knows how you've had a pretty hard time of it and don't want to trust people to treat you well. But, he says that the people close to you know that you're really a good kid who wants to get along with others. He says Santa has so much confidence in you that he's going to *advance* you all the Christmas presents that Santa knows you really deserve."

"I could almost see the wheels turning in his eight year-old head, and you can see the difference in the pictures. Justin hasn't been perfect since Christmas morning, but I definitely think he's been working on a new idea of Christmas. Who knows, this may be the start of a whole new philosophy of life. "

"It is said," Lucy began after a pause, "that Christmas is for kids. This is true insofar as it has the profoundest effect on children and helps them shape their view of what the world is like and their relationship with it. It does help shape their sense of value and justice, and surely contributes to their ethical standards. So, yes, Tanya, a child's idea of Christmas can be a big part of his or her philosophy of life."

"Well, Professor Zhang, I have to say that taking your philosophy classes has helped me think about my own philosophy of Christmas and certainly is helping me identify and clarify my own philosophy of life. Christmas is for adults, too, and philosophy is not only for adults, it's for kids as well. Thank you, so much."

"It was my pleasure, Tanya."

"I hope you always have merry Christmases, Professor Zhang," Tanya said as she left the office, "and a merry life, too."

Lucy whistled "Have Yourself a Merry Little Christmas as she poured herself a steaming cup of tea from her thermos. She was thoroughly tired of hearing Christmas songs for the last two months, but, she thought, "It's never too early to start on next year."

Heartstrings for Christmas

"I *know* what you want for Christmas, Dee. It's *why* you want a violin that I don't know."

"And *I know* what you're saying, Tenisha. Nobody from this side of town should like violin music, and poor girls don't ask for violins for Christmas."

"Girl, I ain't the first one to say it, but Santa don't even have *this* zip code on his list. Especially when it comes to *vio*-lins."

"That's all right, I'm not really going to *ask* for a violin. And I can't help it if I love listening to violin music. Oh, Tenisha, if I could *play* it, nothing else would matter."

Dee went out to catch a bus home from East Riverton Middle School. As she waited, she thought about the holiday concert that was coming up with the Riverton Symphony Orchestra and Chautauqua Churchill. Chautauqua--with whom she was on a first-name basis in her mind--was her idol. She was sixteen, beautiful, and a violin prodigy that *any* girl would gladly trade places with, no matter where she came from.

On the bus ride, the concert stayed in her mind. It wasn't for another six weeks, so there was still hope, but not much, Dee knew. Fifty dollar concert tickets were as much out of the question as a violin. Her mom didn't have a cent to spare for "luxuries," and she, herself, needed every cent she could possibly come up with to get something nice for her mom for Christmas. She believed firmly it was better to give than to receive, and thinking of how hard her mother worked to support them caused a twinge of guilt for feeling even a little sorry for herself.

When she opened the back door of her house, she was greeted by the enthusiastic yapping of the one luxury she had in her life, her dog Cassie and her three pups. Cassie was a Jack Russell beagle mix who she and her mother had the unbelievable luck to have rescued from the animal shelter. The pups were all over her in a fuzzy wave as she let them out of the makeshift corral she and her mom had made for them. She gathered them up one by one, Storm, Frenzy, and her favorite, Violin, and took them and Cassie out into the back yard.

The pups did their thing and alternated chasing and wrestling one other. The girls lived up to their names, and as usual picked on Violin. He was the runt, but he also was irresistibly cute. They *all* were beautiful like their mother. Dee didn't know who their father was, but he must have been one good looking dog to have a paw in creating such pretty pups. They were so pretty that she already had the two girls sold for $25 each, as soon as they were ready to leave their mother.

She called Cassie to her and rubbed her ears. "At least that worked out, girl. I hate to take away your babies, but that extra money will help me buy Mamma something really nice for Christmas. You and I are both gonna be sad, but we'll have each other." Cassie looked at Dee with trusting eyes and what looked like a smile, as if to confirm that everything would be all right.

Dee had already come to terms with losing Storm and Frenzy, but Violin was still a problem. Lovable as he was, he was the first choice of everyone who looked at the puppies. But she pretended he was already promised, hoping somehow that she could keep him. She knew it was unreasonable to think they could afford to feed and take care of two dogs, and she loved Cassie dearly. The thought of giving up Violin, though, was unbearable. She picked him up and cuddled him and let him lick her face, then put that unpleasant thought out of her head.

Instead, she returned to her other violin problem. She thought of the dismal circumstance of her school's having only a band, no orchestra and no string program. If she ever did get a violin, where would she get lessons, and where would she play it? "What I ought to do," she said to Violin, "is write a letter to Chautauqua Churchill and tell her how the kids in the city where she's coming to play will *never* have a chance to do what she's doing."

She held Violin out in front of her face and told him quite seriously, "I'll bet *she* could do something about it." And she began to believe it.

When her mother came in from work, Dee told her that she was thinking of inviting Chautauqua Churchill to come to her school and speak to the students about making something of themselves in life. "She came from poor circumstances, too, Mamma. I could also explain to her about the "no strings" situation at Riverton Middle School and ask her if she would play for a fundraiser to help start a string program.

"What do you think, Mamma? Is this crazy, or what?"

Her mother thought for a few seconds and answered, "I think you're a pretty smart girl; that's what I think. Who knows what might happen? You might, at least, get a free ticket to that concert you want to go to. "

"I didn't know you knew I wanted to go to the concert," Dee said, surprised.

"Mothers know, honey."

"But *that's* not what I'm thinking about, Mamma."

"I know that too, sweetie. I think your idea is terrific. You better get started if you want to try this thing."

***

There was only a week until the concert, and Dee's spirits were dragging on the ground behind her. She hadn't heard anything from Chatauqua Churchill. That meant that she hadn't received a polite note saying "Sorry, Miss Churchill's schedule is full." Worse, she didn't even know if Chatauqua had gotten her letter. "No word" was probably worse than the word "No."

She had given up on going to the concert. The thought had nagged at her that she *had* the money, now that she had sold two of the puppies. She had briefly rethought the idea that it was better to give than to receive, but there really was no way she was going to spend the money for her mother's present on herself.

Storm and Frenzy were gone with two painful goodbyes the week before. With surprisingly little persuasion, her mother had said she could keep Violin until after Christmas. "I want to make sure," Mamma said, "that the people who take him really want a dog and not just an impulsive Christmas present. I want to know they're going to love him and take good care of him."

Dee secretly thought her mother was as good at making up excuses for not giving away Violin as she was. She, of course, couldn't agree more. "But *no one* will take care of him like I would," she told Tenisha more than once. "And there's nobody gonna love him like I do," she said with a sad sigh. She was glad that she got to keep Violin a little longer, but she knew it would be that much worse when she had to give him up. "It's gonna break my heart," she pleaded to her mother, but now her mother was firm. "After

Christmas, he's got to go." Despite this, Dee harbored a small hope that somehow it would work out that she got to keep Violin.

Saturday morning, she and her mom were getting ready to go shopping. They would separate for a while at the mall, and Dee would be able to get her mom's gift. She knew what she was going to buy, but she wanted to check several stores for the best one.

"Honey, come here and sit down for a minute," her mother called from the living room. "I want to tell you something."

Dee sat next to her mother and was heartened when she started with, "I've got some good news for you, sweetie." Dee thought immediately that she was going to say she could keep Violin. But her mom completely surprised her. "You, girl, have a concert to go to tonight."

Dee was completely overwhelmed as her mother continued. "I have heard from the manager of the Riverton Symphony Orchestra, who told me that Miss Chatauqua Churchill asked him to provide you with two tickets."

Dee could not believe what her mother was saying, but there was more." And, she wants to meet you after the concert. So, we'll be shopping today for a proper dress for you to attend the symphony."

***

Dee sat with her mother at the end of the concert, stunned. The concertgoers were making their way out of the theater, but she wasn't moving--not yet, she wanted the experience to go on for as long as possible. For her first concert, the seats they had were fifteen rows back, in the middle. She had a great view of the individual musicians, and the wall of sound had rolled over her, a tidal wave of feelings like the best books she'd read and the best movies she'd seen combined.

The concert had ended with the orchestra's playing holiday favorites. Just before that, Chautauqua Churchill had joined them in a violin concerto by Samuel Barber. As the concerto started, Dee felt as if she were floating above the world, looking down on a story that went from fascinating drama, to almost unbearable sadness, to a frenzied, joyous excitement that reminded her of the two missing puppies. Chautauqua embodied the music. She was beautiful, graceful, powerful, and in command of forces that tapped into Dee's soul. At that moment, Dee was infused with the conviction that she *had* to play the violin and that someday she'd play it like Chautauqua Churchill.

She was thinking that nothing could be better than this when her mother nudged her and said, "Come on, baby, let's go backstage. "Miss Chautauqua Churchill wants to meet my remarkable daughter, and I don't think we should keep her waiting."

They walked up the stairs on the side of the stage and back to where the musicians were laughing and talking and putting away their instruments. Dee was in a daze, but her mother led her confidently to a room, outside of which several people were lined up, including a photographer. While they were waiting, it struck Dee as curious that her mother was so comfortable with all this, as if she already knew everything that was going on. But then she was shaking hands with Chautauqua Churchill and hearing her say, I'm so glad to meet you Dee. Your letter was remarkable."

The rest was a cloud ride that later was hard for her to believe had ever happened. The story in the paper, however, with photos of her and Chautauqua, explained it clearly. Chautauqua was coming back in the spring to play a benefit for her school to jump start a string program and orchestra. Dee was going to have music lessons from one of the Riverton Symphony Orchestra's violinists, and she would practice and play her own violin.

The violin was the best and the most unbelievable part, but she could look at it now, pick it up and run the bow across the strings any time she wanted to make sure it *was* real. That glorious night after the concert, Chautauqua had praised her for her concern for the kids at her school and for her initiative in writing to her. Then, she told Dee that she had heard that she *passionately* wanted to play the violin. Dee had looked over to her mother, and a lot of things started to fall into place. "It just so happens that I have a violin," said Chautauqua, "one of the ones I started playing on, that I've been looking for someone to play who would love it as much as I have."

Dee thought she might faint. Could this really be happening? Chautauqua continued, "But..." and Dee's thought she might have a heart attack instead.

"But, I want something in return. I've been looking for a perfect puppy, not just any puppy, of course, but one that's beautiful and lovable, and loved just as I have loved my violin. I understand you might have such a puppy and might be willing to trade."

It took Dee only a moment to see what was going on and to appreciate what a perfect solution this deal would be. It would give the best of all possible homes for Violin, and she would be trading *love* for *love*.

At this point, Tenisha appeared holding Violin. She gave him to Dee, who snuggled him, kissed him on the head, and said, "I love you, Violin. She turned him over to Chautauqua, who laughed and said, "He *is* perfect."

***

The newspaper article headline read: "Riverton Girl Trades Violin for a Violin." Dee read the article again as she had already read it over and over, as if it were a favorite fantasy story. It was still hard to accept that it wasn't a fantasy and that the girl in the story was her. Dee thought that she would never, ever have an experience so wonderful as this.

There was only one thing that had bothered her. When her mother had told her about the concert and the shopping trip to get a dress, they had spent the money for her mother's present on the dress. She felt that she had betrayed the idea of its being better to give than to receive. It had stayed in the back of her mind, even though it was overcome by all the excitement.

"Mamma, I feel so bad," Dee confesses to her mother on Christmas Eve. "I spent all my Christmas money on myself, on my dress, and I don't have anything to give you for Christmas.'

Her mother hugged her close and said in her best proud mamma voice, "You silly, wonderful girl. Don't you know that you have given me the best Christmas ever?"

Oh Night

"I called this family meeting for now, specifically, because Thanksgiving is our traditional day to get together in our home place. I wanted Thanksgiving itself to be, as much as possible, all it's ever been, and I wanted our heads to be clear, which they definitely are not after the big dinner. So here we are, the day after and *before* leftovers."

Sandy continued, her tone wistful. "You all know what this is about, so I'm going to get right into it. I can't take care of Mom any longer. As you can see, she's gotten worse. She doesn't really respond to anything rationally, and she's still mobile, so someone has to be with her all the time."

Her two brothers listened quietly.

"The day nurse has helped, but even with that, I just can't bear the responsibility anymore. My job is involving as it is, and I'll tell you, I am tired. And speaking of my job, I have an opportunity to move up in the firm, but I'd have to move to the Grand Rapids plant after the first of the year."

"Geez, it seems like . . . heck, it *was* not that long ago she was still singing in her choir and even giving voice lessons," George, the youngest brother offered. "When they talk about rapid onset, they're not kidding."

"And what about this house?" Pat cut in. I know childhood was a long time ago, but, man, there are a lot of happy memories here."

Sandy had expected some avoidance, but she was ready and
 determined to keep on track. "We *will* have to decide about the house, but we need to focus on Mom first. I've done some research, and there's an excellent progressive retirement community not far from here."

***

"Is today the big concert, Andrew?" Judy asked.

"It is," Andy answered his wife's query. "And it's the best gig a social worker and singer could have. I don't know about joy to the world, but joy to these old folks right here is what this Christmas program brings. You can see it and feel it. We're even including the Alzheimer's folks this year, front and center. You remember what I was saying about how research shows that music can sometimes get through to even advanced Alzheimer's folks?"

"Of course I do, dear. You've told me enough times. Say, is your memory getting a little thin?" They had a good laugh at this, and Andy said, "It always has been. Part of my qualification for the job is that I can *empathize* with my clients. I wish you could come to the concert, but I know you can't get off work, and you've seen our show anyway, how many times?"

"Four or five," Judy said smiling. "I'd come anyway if I could. You four guys are so good with everything you do, but your Christmas songs are special."

"We try," Andy averred, "and we're pretty satisfied with what we do. But, you know, I sometimes wish Santa would bring us a female singer. Geoffrey's tenor handles the high parts really well, when we write them in, but a good soprano would be wonderful. Besides, don't you think adding a female to the group would increase our appeal?" He didn't wait for an answer but continued. "Are you sure you don't want to take voice lessons and join us?"

Judy chuckled with mock appreciation. "Oh yeah, that would help all right, adding a squeaky wheel to your well-oiled machine."

"Well, at least I'd have a pretty girl in the group I could hit on," Andy said, smiling widely.

"Listen, Buster, that's exactly why you *don't* need a female in the group. If you need to prop up your maleness, you can sing to me right here. You know that'll work."

***

The scene was bustling in the big main dining room at Oakdale Commons as the staff made final preparations for the annual Christmas program. The big round tables had been folded up and moved to the back, and the padded chairs were arranged in rows and others added to accommodate all the guests. Friends and family mingled with the residents with holiday spirit that was generally festive. Sandy sat with her mother in the front row. Most of the front row residents also had husbands or wives, adult children, or even a few grandchildren sitting with them, an arrangement that allowed them to interact as they could and freed up staff.

Sandy had driven from Grand Rapids especially for the program. She was pleased with everything she had seen and heard so far today, as she pretty much had been over the past year. Her mother had a compact private suite, with a bedroom, bathroom, and sitting room with a window that looked out onto trees and a fringe of lawn. The green was gone from both, but she knew it would be pleasant when the spring returned. There was also a shelving unit on one wall with a TV and a music player and room for pictures and memorabilia. At one end of this was a writing desk with room to slide in a wheelchair below, and a memo board on which patient or staff could write the day's schedule. Sandy thought the last was a nice touch and might even be therapeutic in some ways.

She was disappointed and a not a little angry that her brothers claimed to be too busy to come to the Christmas program. She knew from a year's experience that her brothers still considered her to be primarily responsible for visiting their mother. She was, after all, by their logic the closest. A three-hour-plus drive or a half-day plane hop, though, was hardly close. She was especially annoyed because her brothers knew how much her mother had been invested in music, and music was the most important element of the Christmas program. The program was supposed to include a set by a local acapella group that had a good reputation and included the Oakdale social worker responsible for her mother. The fact that her brothers didn't *want* to share this with their mother, who had shared so much with them, really ticked her off.

Before the program, Sandy chatted with her mother next to her with only a smile in response. The woman sitting on the other side of her, next to her own father, introduced herself as Donna and her father as Ray. Ray acknowledged the introduction brightly with, "Good neighborhood, cul-de-sac." Then his eyes closed and his chin went back on his chest, a position that Sandy had grown used to among residents on the Alzheimer's floor.

Sandy wondered for a second if Ray was referring to Oakdale, but Donna cleared that up with, "Dad was quite successful in real estate before. You have to watch out or he'll try to sell you a house, four bedrooms, three baths, great schools, and all." She said it laughing, and Sandy decided she liked her attitude.

"Mom," Sandy said, "This is Donna and Ray. Donna and Ray, this is my mother, Helen."

"I'm pleased to meet you, Helen," Donna said pleasantly. Neither Ray nor Sandy's mother acknowledged the introduction.

Helen, instead, looked straight ahead, her eyes open and a smile on her face, as if everything were fine in her world. The trouble was that this was her countenance most of the time, regardless of what was going on around her. This was poignant, Sandy had long since concluded, better than an unhappy or blank look. She even thought that maybe there was music running through her mother's mind all the time causing the smile, and she was good with that.

"Mom was a home maker, and she did make a wonderful home," Sandy continued the introduction. "She volunteered a lot, too, with school music programs. She also gave private singing lessons and sang in several choirs. I hope—and I believe—that she's really looking forward to this program."

Sandy and Donna further related their parent's stories with the immediate intimacy of shared misfortune. Ray's dementia had come on more slowly than Helen's. He had, however, become more and more agitated over his loss of control over his life. His insistence on trying to sell real estate to anyone and everyone, including family members, had become increasingly annoying and aggressive, until Oakdale had become the best alternative for him. He continued intermittently to offer great properties to the other residents, but the staff could expertly talk him down if he became too insistent.

Sandy told how her mother's problems had developed quickly, and how she had gone to live with Helen and tried to balance helping her and keeping her job. Hiring a day nurse had helped, and her mother was easy to get along with, even as she became more and more distant. In the end, however, she just couldn't handle it by herself. She felt at ease talking with Donna in a way she didn't with most people. She knew she didn't have to apologize or justify her decision to not be a full-time caretaker to someone in the same position as she was.

Then the show was ready to begin. The Oakdale director stepped up onto the makeshift stage and tapped the microphone sharply. Sandy suspected it was as much to get the attention of all the Brookdale residents as it was to test the microphone. The director thanked everyone for being there—an irony that wasn't lost on most of them—and especially those family and friends who had interrupted their schedules or come a long way to be with their loved ones for the holidays.

"You are in for a treat today. We have bells; we have Christmas readings, both religious and secular; we have a play written and performed by our Oakdale theater group; and we have, for the fourth year in a row, the wonderful acapella group, Message. I'll turn it over now to our own Marjorie Mitchell, who will introduce the performers. Sit back and enjoy."

Sandy was puzzling over the director's pronunciation as an attractive, silver-haired woman stepped up and told a few insider jokes that got some good laughs, especially from the residents who were getting into a festive spirit.

"She's really quite funny," Donna said to Sandy, who welcomed the injection of humor and agreed. Raymond lifted his head and asked, "What'd she say?" rather too loudly. Sandy looked at her mother, who appropriately looked straight ahead and smiled, like a broken clock that's right twice a day.

The program progressed merrily with Christmas tunes from the bell ringers, young people from a nearby church. They were followed by residents who recited "The Night Before Christmas" and the Bible Christmas story. Then, a man and woman from a local Jewish congregation did an exemplary job of delivering *The Story of Hanukkah*. The woman sat in a chair and read Amy Ehrlich's children's picture book in a strong, clear voice while the man stood and showed the pictures. Then a man and woman lit 12 candles onstage for each of the Kwaanza principles and explained each. The audience seemed to enjoy both the information and the ecumenism of it.

This was followed by the ten-minute skit that the theater group had collectively written and had been rehearsing for weeks. The story line had to do with an older man and an older woman, alone for Christmas, who found each other through a somewhat contrived set of circumstances. It was, nonetheless, sweet and the audience ate it up.

Marjorie Mitchell kept it all moving smoothly between presenters. After the play, she announced a short intermission, during which Christmas cookies and apple cider would be brought around for everyone to enjoy. Sandy appreciated the opportunity to get up and stand.

"How did you like the program so far?" she asked her mother. Helen smiled, a good sign, Sandy thought, under normal circumstances, but no sign at all in the present. She chatted with Donna and tried to involve her mother and Raymond, too, in the conversation, but to no avail. She really hoped, regardless, that some of this was getting through to Helen and that it was actually a positive experience for her.

Marjorie Mitchell returned to the stage to introduce the featured acapella group. "And now, we come to the main musical part of our program. For the fourth year in a row, we are very privileged to have the beautiful harmonies of Message, featuring our own *master* social worker—and I don't just mean MSW—Andy Washington.

The audience exploded in applause, and Sandy leaned over and said to Donna, "I thought this group was called Message.

Donna laughed and told her, "It's spelled like "message," but it rhymes with "massage."

"I like it," Sandy returned, smiling. "I hope they can deliver on both."

"We are Message," Andy said from center stage, "and we love to be here singing for you again. There is a whole lot of experience here and good memories of the holiday season. We ask you to tap into that experience and those memories as we give you some of the songs of the season." And the music began.

The group started with "Let It Snow," and conveniently through the wall of windows that looked out onto a courtyard, snow was coming down lightly, but in big flakes. A perfect setting, thought Andy, for this song to take residents off to other happy places they'd been. Many in the audience were looking at the falling snow. There was also a smattering of closed eyes, but not from dozing off, rather from people envisioning other snowy places along the road to this time and place.

Message continued with "Jingle Bells" and other bright and cheery secular songs. Their voices blended like oil and vinegar in open harmonies; dark blue ties and light blue shirts in closed harmonies; and the chef, cooks, and wait staff in a fine restaurant in polyphonic phrases. They rocked the house with a mashup of "Rockin' Around the Christmas Tree," "Jingle Bell Rock," and "Frosty the Snowman."

After Frosty had hopped off over the fields of snow, Andy introduced the singers. "On my right is our bass/baritone Jerry Rodriguez. Next to him is our tenor, George Lassiter. On my right is baritone D'Juan Chavis. And I am a baritone, Andy Watson. Together we are Message."

Warm applause swept over them. When it let up, Andy continued. "We call ourselves Message because we hope our music has something to say, and we hope it relaxes and pleases you. Here we go."

The program switched to more reverent religious classics. "Do You Hear What I Hear" provided a neat transition and gave the lower voices a chance to do some beat boxing while Geoffrey's tenor carried the melody line. They followed up with "Oh Come All Ye Faithful"; "Little Drummer Boy"; a spirited, folky Hanukkah song, "Don't Let the Light Go Out"; and "Angels We Have Heard on High." The followup, "The Kwanzaa Song," featuring D'Juan in the lead, smooth and very rhythmic at the same time earned an appreciative response.

"Our last song, Andy announced will be "Oh Night." We invite you to sing along if you like." They started with a wordless introduction, then sang the first verse. A few of the audience members joined in tentatively. The second verse began, and a bit scratchy soprano voice joined in. Helen looked over to her mother, amazed that she was singing! As she went on, her voice increased in clarity and intensity. By the third phrase of the verse, she was singing full on. When the song reached the last phrase and the high notes of 'Oh night divine,' she was soaring.

Everyone in the group was shocked and amazed except Andy. He had a huge smile that nearly disrupted his articulation, and he looked at each of the other singers and nodded as if to say, "Okay, boys, here's a soprano; Let's see what we can do." They continued on, with renewed inspiration.

Sandy couldn't take her eyes off her mother, who had stood up and was singing, quite literally, at the top of her voice. Call it muscle memory or whatever, she was putting her whole breath into it and projecting amazingly for someone who hadn't sung a note for two years and had been sitting passively minutes ago. Helen had had a clear, warm lyric soprano voice quality before, and she did again. The visitors in the audience were appreciatively astonished at the beauty of the sound. The residents were even more stunned. On the final 'Oh night, Andy stepped out a bit and with upheld palms signaled the group to hold the high note until Helen broke it. And indeed, she held it for eight beats before descending gracefully to the last words.

An awed silence followed for a full five seconds for an audience that didn't want the song to end and wasn't sure what had just happened. Then, the applause exploded, along with various calls of approval. The singers on stage were also applauding vigorously, looking in Helen's direction.

Helen sat down and smiled.

Home for Christmas

Theodore Farley drummed his fingers on the steering wheel. He'd never done this kind of thing before. His eyes swept the four corners ahead and the streets leading up to them as far as he could see. He watched for police cruisers or the outside chance car of someone who might know him. Mostly though, he searched for a certain young woman.

He knew the woman, or the "girl" as he thought of her, worked this intersection regularly. He'd observed her many times in the past three or four months as he drove home from work. A wildflower he thought of her, springing from the cracked sidewalks and dirty storefronts. The artificial light from the bar, the liquor store, and the pawn shop made the setting a greenhouse for noxious weeds, which made this girl the more beautiful and, he thought, the more out of place.

It was only a little earlier than he usually came through here, wanting to be sure not to miss her, but his tenseness made it seem like forever. "Maybe she isn't working tonight," he thought with both disappointment and relief. "Or maybe she's already gone off with someone," and his feelings switched to compassion and regret. The emotion cycle continued with panic as the question renewed itself, "What if one of the others comes up and talks to me? What will I say?"

"God, it *is* Christmas Eve," flashed, next, and that was enough, like releasing a parking brake, to reduce the whole thing to absurdity. His eyes quickly took in the intersection once more, and he put the idling car into gear and pulled away from the curb. "This is insane," he said out loud. "It'll never work out, just a waste of time." He hadn't gone half a block though before he started going over the plan again in his head.

His intention was to prove how naïve and fantastic it was, but the effect was just the opposite. It was all there, simple and appealing, just as he had worked it out, bit by bit, over the past month. Ever since he had first noticed her on that corner, he had known that he had to do something. She looked to be no more than a child. He had read about runaways as young as twelve or thirteen getting into "the profession."

At the next intersection, Farley turned sharply right, went over a block, back three, and right again.

One more right and he was back to his previous spot. As he pulled over, he saw her walking on the cross street towards the intersection. She didn't have to get close for him to know it was her. He'd seen her in the streetlight many times.

"She's so pretty," he thought now, "or she would be without all that makeup." He hadn't seen her closer than on the sidewalk as he drove by, but he knew she was beautiful. He imagined he knew many things about her, but in actuality, he realized he knew nothing.

Farley turned his lights on and off several times in what he thought was a good signal. She crossed the street and casually walked up to and past his car. He was surprised she didn't stop, but his eyes fell to his side-view mirror, and he tracked her as she turned tentatively, then came briskly back to his window. The window came down quickly, despite his trembling hands.

"Are you looking for something, Mister?" She leaned over the open window and smiled. Farley couldn't exactly decode the smile, but he thought he saw sadness in it. He smiled back, himself genuinely happy to finally be talking to her. His heart was pounding, and he took in a deep breath before responding. Drawing it in, one impression was confirmed, "She *is* beautiful, and she is a child—sixteen or seventeen." But her beauty was clouded as much by pain as it was by makeup.

"Listen, pal, what'll it be," she demanded. "I don't have all night" As Farley still hesitated, she retorted herself, "Actually, I *do* have all night, but it will cost you," but completely without humor.

Taking this as glibness nonetheless, Farley finally got out, "I have a proposition for you."

"Uh huh. You and every other horny toad out there. My question is, what *is* it?"

Farley realized this really *wasn't* going to work if he didn't get a chance to tell it clearly and convincingly, so he started again. "First, tell me your name."

She looked at Farley as if he were crazy, but answered, "Susie."

"Look Susie, this is a little complicated and it's not what you think it is. I need to explain to you what I want, and it isn't anything weird or harmful. Get in and I'll give you twenty dollars to listen for a few minutes. If you don't like what I have to say, I'll give you twenty more and that will be that."

"Give me the twenty first, and then I'll get in."

Farley's nervousness diminished some. He thought he had her now that she was negotiating. Negotiation was part of what he did for a living, so they were on solid ground together. "Mmm, and what's to keep you from just taking off with the twenty?"

Susie rose to the challenge, "Well, what's to keep you from taking off with *me* once I get in."

"Fair enough," Farley conceded. Thinking it was reasonably safe since he had a spare key in his wallet, he agreed. "I'll turn off the car and give you the keys. You get in and I'll give you the twenty"

Susie took the keys, came around, and got in the car. "Okay, you talk. I'll listen, but I'll tell you right now there are some things I won't do."

"First," Farley began, "Tell me your name so I can address you properly."

"I told you, Susie."

He cocked his head, frowned, caught her eyes and held them. She looked back and after a few seconds said without explanation, "Laura, Laura Ann."

"Laura, I'm Ted Farley, and I *am* genuinely pleased to meet you. I've been seeing you here for a while. I come this way from work."

He almost said, "And I want to help you," but he caught himself. "I want to take you home to dinner," and he immediately knew while that didn't sound patronizing, it did sound pretty weird.

Laura put her hand on the door handle, and he hurried to finish, "To Christmas dinner with me and my wife."

She looked at him with a mix of skepticism and curiosity and said, "Go on."

Farley couldn't remember what he was supposed to say next. He looked past her and saw that snow had begun to fall gently and that several patrons were about to go through an arch of Christmas lights into the bar. He laughed silently at these incongruous signs of the season and the juxtaposition he was about to propose seemed less strange.

"My wife and I are fifty-five years old. Our son was killed in Iraq. Our daughter lives in California. She and her family are going away for Christmas. It's going to be just the two of us this year in a big house in the suburbs. Christmas isn't what it used to be. We thought it would be great to have a young person over to share the day with, to laugh and celebrate."

He succeeded in saying it calmly, as if it were the most reasonable thing in the world. He thought he hadn't let in a trace of pity or let on that what he and his wife really wanted was to help her. He thought this just might work.

Laura took a moment to evaluate this, her lips pressed together and her brow lowered. Then, her response came angry and accusing. "Mister, I haven't been happy for a long time, and the only thing I celebrate is making enough money to eat."

She regretted saying it when she saw the sadness in his eyes. Somehow, she couldn't hate this well-off man, the way she hated all men, the way she hated the cruel and abusive father she had escaped from.

"Look." Farley said, "This will be as new experience for all of us. I think it will be a good one, but there are no strings attached." Except, he thought, for the ones around the packages he and his wife had already wrapped for her. "If you feel uncomfortable, you can leave any time. I'll take you back to wherever you want to go. But please consider it. You'd be doing a big favor for me and for my wife."

"Laura's head spun with confusion. She looked out the window at her sordid environment. It was definitely a place to get away from, even for a day, but the animal instinct that helped her survive in the streets threw up a red flag. This offer threatened somehow the tiny bit of independence she had achieved at such a high cost. On the other hand, she had learned to grab at any advantage she could.

Maybe she could get a good meal and that would be that. Another voice raised the question: Why would Mr. and Mrs. Ted respectable Farley want someone like her for a dinner guest?

She turned to challenge him, but the kindness and concern on his face answered her question. Still, she knew she'd feel uncomfortable, out of place, and she thought of *My Fair Lady* she'd once seen on TV.

Mentally, she edged toward the door, but her body didn't move. She was shouting in her head, "Why don't you leave me alone?" But her lips only quivered. A feeling of just wanting to go home washed over her. But she didn't have a home. Then she thought of how *My Fair Lady* ended and how it made her feel good.

Farley said, "Shall I pick you up in the morning?" It brought the decision she had to make back into focus.

"Mr. Farley," she started, considering as she spoke, "I'm not sure why, but I think you're telling the truth." She paused for a moment, and the logic of the situation finally struck her.

"I guess I don't have anything to lose," she said, as much to herself as to him. "There's only one thing. The rest was tearful. "Take me home tonight. I love Christmas Eve."

A River Runs Through It

♪I'll be home for Christmas...♪

Man, the first few times it was poignant, but this is getting to be too much. That has to be the fourth or fifth time I've heard that song since this morning.

That's what you get, dumbass, for keeping it on "The Sounds of Christmas" the whole way.

Like there is something else on.

Well, don't complain then. You wanted to immerse yourself in Christmas. You wanted to go home for Christmas.

I know, I know. But Christ!

Geez, I wish I could break myself of saying that. Reason enough that I don't believe in that stuff, but given the season, it's completely ironic. Or moronic.

That's it, keep it light. We want this to be a Christmas to remember.

Oh, your capacity for irony slays me.

Good one, but you ain't seen nothing yet.

I guess, but isn't that a little bit freaky?

Ironic.

Freaky.

Okay, ironic *and* freaky.

Riverside exit fourteen miles. The old stomping grounds.

Uh huh, but I'll bet it's changed.

I'll bet it's changed a lot.

Nevertheless, it's home.

♪I'll be home for Christmas, if only in my dreams♪

***

Holy shit, look at all that development. It looks like goddam mall world. Man, before they put the freeway through, there wasn't even a *gas station* here. Now, it looks as if the town has expanded to meet the freeway.

I hope the downtown is still thriving. Look, there's what used to be Andy's Saloon. I always wanted to know what went on inside Andy's. The rumors...

Now you'll never know. You won't know forever.

Minor stuff, insignificant. Let's go by the high school.

**

They don't make 'em like that anymore. There's nothing like a three- story brick school house.

Right and right. They don't make three-story brick schoolhouses anymore, and there *is* nothing like 'em, including this one. It's not a school anymore.

Hmm...

Remember the Snow Ball, junior year?

Oh god, yes. That white gown, those sequins, her frosted hair. Janie darling, you were the princess of new fallen snow on a sunny morning—too utterly perfect to trespass.

But you did, fool, you asked her to dance.

And she did say yes.

And she did say yes. The first time, huh?

The first of many yesses. Oh Janie, you were so agreeable. So positive.

Then, that smile passing in the hall. Absolute magic. It transformed you from nobody to somebody with the holiest purpose in the world—to win her love. You were Don Quixote and knew it.

I expected to get hurt but didn't care. I wonder what she saw in me then? How could any woman so perfect end up loving *me*?

I truly don't know. I've often wondered that myself. When you'd ask her, she'd only laugh.

Ah, that laugh. There was never more beautiful music.

You thought she would laugh when you asked her out. Wait, she did laugh, or at least she smiled over the phone. And she said yes.

The rest is history.

History. We all are history, waiting for time to write upon us. Like the river to the sea, never to return, taking life with it.

Oh my, how eloquent.

Life is poetry. You just have to see it. Right to the end.

***

Well, downtown hasn't changed that much. Actually, it's looking pretty good. Oh no, look at that. Brown's Drugs is now a Rite Aid. That's kind of sad.

As goes Brown's Drugs, so goes the world. I guess that's what they mean when they say you can't go home again.

Come on, we went through all this before and we decided to come.

You know, it almost would have been better if this were a ghost town and this downtown deserted.

It *is* a ghost town; there are ghosts all around. Look, there's Janie.

Hmm, yeah. We used to hang out with the other kids at Brown's soda fountain. I'll tell you, those were the days. Brown let us alone and we appreciated it. No rules, but we knew our limits were.

Uh huh, like no public displays of affection. You and Janie broke that one a few times.

For sure, but we were discreet. We displayed our affection when no one was looking.

And how do you know that? You weren't looking either.

Mmmm...yeah.

I wonder if the soda fountain is still there. Should we go in and look?

Nah, it's almost surely gone. So let's *not* go in and pretend it's still there.

We're pretty good at pretending. Let's go check out if Shorty's is still there instead.

***

Hey, it's still The Sandwich Shop. That's cool. But I'll bet Shorty isn't there anymore. You want to see?

Sure, why not. I wouldn't mind having one of Shorty's Specials. Best damn sandwich in the world. It can be our last meal before leaving this burg forever.

There's a parking spot!

***

"Hey, Shorty! I can't believe you're still here!"

"Riley McDonald! Well, I'll be. Sometimes I can't believe I'm still here either. How are you, Riley?"

I'm still living, Shorty."

"That's great. You know, everyone who's been here forever is proud that you *used to* be here. Not many people from Riverside ever get to be famous. How's the writing going?"

"I'd hardly call myself famous, Shorty. Poet's don't get to be famous. All they get to do is hope that a few people here and there see something they've written, and some of those like what they read."

Well, son, you can count me in that select group. I've read all your books, and I like them a lot. Do you know you've got me turned on to poetry? It takes some work, but it's like one of my specials—you like the taste, so you want to find out what it's made out of. Your stuff is easier to understand because I know you. In fact, I think I know you better now than when you used to come in here all the time."

"Shorty, I know myself better. I am so flattered that you've taken the time to read my work."

"Riley, your very best stuff is written for Jane. I'm really, really sorry to hear about her. Are you all right, boy?"

"Shorty, Janie made a *man* out of me a long time ago. I have a new book coming out dedicated entirely to her. I'm sure you'll hear about it very soon."

"I will definitely look for it. Hey, what can I get for you, Riley? It's not on the menu at the moment, but I can make you your favorite."

"That would be fantastic."

***

Well, that was pleasant. I'm glad we stopped. Shorty always was a great guy, and we surely did have some good times there. If I could go back…

What for? You certainly wouldn't change anything. Hell, man you were lucky. If your tried it all over, you'd almost surely screw it up, and you wouldn't have had the times you did.

I know, I know.

The point is, you can't go back.

Nevertheless, it's time to go back to the old home place.

***

Be it ever so humble...I so wish Mom hadn't sold it. I mean, I realize it was easier for her to live closer to Rosie. But so much *happened* here. This is where I proposed to Janie! On this very date, December 23. In this very place.

That's why we're here.

But there's more. Not much more, it's true, but what's left is essential. It's the last line that makes the whole story work.

***

Janie's house. We lived so close for so many years but so very far away.

You loved her for a long time, but she never knew until...

Until I asked her to dance. If I hadn't gotten up the nerve, history would have changed.

His story, her story. She was your world. World history would have been altered.

From the best of all possible worlds.

Why in the world did her parents move away too? It's as if no one wants to call Riverside home.

But Janie did. And I did. Now we can call it home forever. Look at how big those spruce trees have grown. It's so cool how they've kept up the tradition of putting lights on them. She would have loved it.

A Christmas tree for Janie.

***

There's the river.

And there's the bridge.

I hope we can find a place to park close by. I want to raise as little curiosity as possible over why we're on the bridge and what we're doing. This is a solemn and solitary thing we're about.

Holy.

Truly holy. Look, they've built a park here, right on the river and close to the bridge.

Just a short walk, and even a walkway.

***

This is perfect no fence or anything. The guard rail is easily accessible.

Geez, it's cold.

But no wind and no ice. An early freeze would have messed up everything.

Okay, we're about in the middle. Up on the rail before anyone comes along.

Janie, this will have to be brief. Everything I've ever wanted to say to you is in the book.

First her ashes. "River, I give to you the woman I love."

Now me. "Janie, this is my Christmas present to you. I join you with my heart and soul to diffuse with you into the waters of life."

And he threw the book.

Kiss in Play

Ryan Reynolds was glum. He should have been happy; it was Christmas break. But there just wasn't enough drama in his life. The first five days of freedom from school had been completely free of drama—in more ways than one. His social life was non-existent. What there was of it, with the drama club, was at a low point. The last performance of the South Rockford High Drama Club's spring musical and the cast party were history a week and a half ago. There wouldn't be another drama club meeting for three weeks. The next production wouldn't be until the annual Christmas play.

Drama club was shy Ryan's only means for social interaction with other South Rockford kids. Actually, he mostly interacted with Ms. Jenkins, the club's sponsor and the few other students on the set construction crew. But being in Drama Club allowed him to be close to Kay Connor and to imagine himself playing next to her. She always had a speaking role in their productions; he always watched from the wings.

Kay was the love of Ryan's life and the biggest vacuum in it. He excelled at everything academic, math and science especially, but that was hardly cause for popularity at South Rockford. Kay was also brainy: brainy, beautiful, and an extrovert—a much more effective formula for social success. Ryan had her in Algebra II and Pre-calculus, and she was nice enough to him, but she was nice to everyone. He could only dream of love; doing something to bring it about was beyond his ability. But dreaming and doing were about to come together for Ryan—at least in writing.

As he sat there glumly, Ryan was playing with a pencil and it came into his head that maybe he should write a poem and give it to Kay. "God, a poem," he thought, however. "That's a sure way to prove nerdiness. Won't work." He continued to toy with the pencil, but his thoughts kept going back to the Christmas play. "If only I could play alongside of her in a production. . . If only I could write myself into her life. . ." Being an intelligent and ingenious young man, he made a start.

A KISS BEGINS WITH KAY
_____

A Play in Two Acts
By Ryan Reynolds

Cast of Characters

Ryan Reynolds/Peter   A shy, very intelligent
high school junior and understudy/male lead in a
Christmas play.

Ryan's mother

Katherine Conrad/Shawna   An outgoing, intelligent
high school junior and female lead in a Christmas
play.

Katherine's mother

Phyllis Jenkins   High school drama
teacher.

Jay Spencer   High school senior and
                        male lead in a Chris
Christmas play.

Other cast members   Various high school
students in the play.

Scene
Various locations in South Rockford, a small
suburban community.

Time

The present.

ACT I

Scene 1

SETTING: Stage left, Ryan's living room.
Stage right, Katherine's living room.

AT RISE: Stage left, Ryan and his mother in
conversation.
Stage right, Katherine and her mother in
conversation.

RYAN
I'll be getting home late this afternoon, Mom. Drama
Club is having a meeting to discuss the Christmas
play.

RYAN'S MOTHER
Oh! Already? Okay, thanks for letting me know, Ryan.
Call me at work if you need to.

KATHERINE
Mom, Guess what. The Christmas play is going to be
romantic comedy, and there's an awesome female
lead.

KATHERINE'S MOTHER
That's great, Katherine. I don't suppose you're
interested in being the star.

KATHERINE
We'll see, Mom. We'll see.

(BLACKOUT)

(LIGHTS UP)
(Three weeks later)

(Stage left)
RYAN'S MOTHER
Wow, Ryan! You're going to try out for the lead?
That's a big step. I know you've worked on building
sets and such, but acting and the lead?

RYAN
You're not exactly building my confidence, Mother. It
won't hurt to try out. I've been observing and
analyzing what goes into acting, and I've got it pretty
well figured out. And if I do get it, it will look great on
my application to MIT.

RYAN'S MOTHER
I'm not being negative, Honey. I'm just a little
surprised. Is Katherine Crawford going to be in this
play?

RYAN
Uh, maybe. Why do you ask?

RYAN'S MOTHER
Don't you have a tiny crush on her?

RYAN

Come on, Mom. A macro-popular girl like Kay isn't going to have anything to do with a nano-nerd guy like me. You know I try to be realistic.

RYAN'S MOTHER
All right. But *is* she trying out for the play, and maybe for the female lead?

RYAN
Yes, she is, and you know she has it sewn up.

(Stage right)
KATHERINE'S MOTHER
So, you like the role, Katherine? The female lead would be terrific. What are your chances? Who else is trying out?

KATHERINE
It would be a lot of fun, and actually, no one else is trying out that I know of. Ms. Jenkins is trying to interest one of the sophomore girls to understudy. But you never know what might happen. And you'd never guess who's trying out for the male lead. It's Ryan Reynolds. And Jay Spencer, of course.

KATHERINE'S MOTHER
Well, Jay is about as sure a thing as you are. Does Ryan have any chance?

KATHERINE
Oh my god, no. But... you know he's really smart. There's no one in the school as smart. And he's really endeared himself to Ms. Jenkins with his ideas for

sets and stage direction. But, no, it's not going to happen.

Mother nods knowingly with a wisp of a smile on her lips.

(CURTAIN)
END OF SCENE)

<u>ACT I</u>

(Scene 2)

SETTING: Rockford H.S. stage.

AT RISE: Cast members are scattered about and chatting. Ms. Jenkins is center stage, standing by enough chairs to accommodate cast. She calls out to cast members.

PHYLLIS JENKINS
All right, bring your scripts and have a seat. Today, I want to read the final act. Kay and Jay, this is where it all comes together for Shawna and Peter—both figuratively and literally—but we'll discuss that last scene when we get to it.

Ryan, I know I don't need to say it, but pay close attention. You know I wish you had auditioned for a smaller part for your first speaking role, and there is no chance with only two performances that you'll get to say a word. But being understudy to Jay is a terrific opportunity to learn, so take full advantage of it.

Ryan is visibly chafed at this.

(Cast sits on chairs. Ms. Jenkins stands and directs as they read the script but without vocalizing. After about a minute of this, vocalizing begins.

PHYLLIS JENKINS
Good. Good. That brings us to the last scene. Shawna and Peter have made peace with one another, and they are front and center at rise. The cast is stage rear, and the scene is the cast party. Shawna says to Peter . . .

KATHERINE
Oh Peter, I am so happy that we finally have gotten to know each other as we really are.

PHYLLIS JENKINS
They look deeply into one another's eyes and embrace.
The script, as you see, calls for a kiss here. I've checked with the administration, and a quote unquote, "reasonably chaste" kiss would be all right. However, the actuality will be up to the actors involved. Kay and Jay, your choices are a simple embrace, a stage kiss with no lips touching, or that reasonably chaste kiss. You need to come to an agreement beforehand, although it may turn out that what ends up happening will be spontaneous, depending on how deeply you both are into your roles.

Also, after the "kiss," the curtain will close briefly, but you all will maintain your positions. It will open again, and the entire cast will come forward, and all will wish the audience "Merry Christmas."

Okay, we will read the script through at out next meeting, and then we will start with full rehearsals. See you all next time.

(CURTAIN)
(END OF SCENE)

ACT II

(Scene 1)

SETTING: South Rockford H.S. auditorium, opening performance of Christmas play, Friday night.

AT RISE: Stage is set for the final scene of the Christmas play. Cast party is underway on the back half of the stage, with the entire cast vocally having fun. (Katherine and Jay as Shawna and Peter are on the front side of the group
talking and gesturing toward the front of the stage. Holding hands, they move away from the party to center stage front. As they move, the part noise fades to quiet and the rear stage lights dim. Shawna and Peter join hands and look into one another's eyes.)

PETER (Jay)
I guess what they say about Christmas bringing people together, at least for a day, is true.

SHAWNA (Katherine)
Oh Peter, I'm so glad we've gotten to know each other for real by acting in a play. I'm sure it won't be for just a day, either.

(Slowly, they come together and "kiss." On this night, Katherine turns her head slightly so that their lips fall on each other's cheek. The curtain closes and the entire cast comes forward and calls out . . .)

CAST
Merry Christmas!

(CURTAIN)
(END OF SCENE)

ACT II

Scene 2

SETTING: Ms. Jenkins's home, Saturday morning.

AT RISE: Ms. Jenkins "hangs up" her phone, obviously in great consternation.

PHYLLIS JENKINS
Oh God, it's a good thing he didn't kiss her last night.

("Dials" her phone)

Ryan? Oh good. I was afraid I wouldn't be able to get hold of you. Listen, Jay has the flu. He's throwing up all over the place and feel like he's gonna die. You know what this means. Are you ready to be Peter?

Good boy. Look, I'd like you to come over to the auditorium at noon so we can read through the script and go over where you need to be on stage and all that.

I know, I know, you have it all down, but humor me. I'm the one who needs to go over things.

Good, see you there.

(Hangs up her phone)

I just hope the rest of the kids don't come down with this before tonight. I better call to alert them to what's going on.

(Starts calling the rest of the cast and crew.)

(CURTAIN)
END OF SCENE)

ACT II
Scene 3

SETTING: South Rockford H.S. auditorium, second play performance, Saturday night.

AT RISE: Stage light on only at rear. Ms. Jenkins is giving pep talk to cast.

PHYLLIS JENKINS
(*very much the coach, with passion*)
I can't give you all enough praise for the job you are
doing tonight. Ryan, you've been great! We may all be
in the hospital tomorrow, but tonight *we are
troupers*! Let's bring this last scene to the finish and
go to the cast party in glory!

(Jenkins exits and cast takes places for final scene)

(Curtain closes and opens)

ACT II
Scene 4

SETTING: Final performance, Saturday night.

AT RISE: Cast party is underway on back half of
stage with entire cast vocally having fun.

(Katherine and Ryan as Shawna and Peter are on the
front side of the group
talking and gesturing toward the front of the stage.
Holding hands, they move away from the party to
center stage front. As they move, the part noise fades
to quiet and the rear stage lights dim. Shawna and
Peter join hands and look into one another's eyes.)

PETER (Ryan)
I guess what they say about Christmas bringing
people together, at least for a day, is true.

SHAWNA (Katherine)

Oh Peter, I'm so glad we've gotten to know each other for real by acting in a play. I'm sure it won't be for just a day, either.

(Slowly they come together, and Katherine ad libs)

SHAWNA

Oh, kiss me, Peter.

(Ryan looks at her, nonplussed, for a second, and they kiss full on.

(The curtain closes briefly, and when it reopens, Katherine and Ryan are still kissing. The cast behind them holds its "Merry Christmas." A little embarrassed Katherine and Ryan stop kissing.)

(Entire cast comes forward and bows. As Katherine and Ryan take their bow together, the cast takes up a chant of "Encore, encore." Hopefully the audience takes up the chant.)

(Katherine and Ryan comply.)

(CURTAIN)
(END OF SCENE)

ACT II

Scene 5

SETTING: Ryan's living room.

AT RISE: Ryan is sitting at a table writing.

(He looks up from the pages in front of him and smiles.)

RYAN
Okay, I know it needs a lot of work, but things are going to be different next year.

FINAL CURTAIN

Twelve Stories

of Christmas

About The Author

Chris Brockman

Chris Brockman is retired from teaching both middle school Language Arts and community college English and writing. He writes and posts an original poem weekly on his Real Poetry for Real People Facebook page. The stories herein were written over many years just for pleasure.

Books By This Author

Growing Up in Boom Times

Even as we Baby Boomers have put our stamp on our world, our growing up has had a profound effect on us. We rebelled, protested, turned on. We bridged the simplicity of our parents' youth and the beguiling complexity of our own children's. Before all that, though, we played outside a lot and without fear, we ate dinner at home with our families, we found good things to watch on our three or four T.V. channels, and we managed to have great fun close to home with just our bikes, our dogs, and our friends.

I Used to Be Old

Accessible themed poetry on the ups and downs of aging.

Life in Brief

Wind and sun and rain and earth,

Ideas, ideals, work and mirth.

The garden grows, and life sustains.

Love and laughter trump sorrow and pain.

We're born, we grow, we live, we die.

Hello, how are you, I'm fine, good bye.

Along the way we celebrate.

Our genes, our dreams we propagate.

When we go, we go content

With value bought in hours spent.

What to Think about: Philosophy for a Thoughtful Younger Generation

In What to Think About: Philosophy for a Thoughtful Younger Generation, Chris Brockman uses his own definition of "philosophy" as a "systematic study of who I am, what's out there, and what should I do about it" to arrive at suggestions for things to think about. Each chapter ends with scenarios and questions challenging the reader to think. This book is "written from a humanist perspective," and may offend some religious sensibilities. It is recommended for young adults.

Malachi's Cove

Illustrated adaptation of a classic Anthony Trollope story as a young adult chapter book. Young Mally Trenglos gathers seaweed from a roiling Cornwall cove to sell to farmers for fertilizer to support her aged grandfather. When a local farmer's son tries to infringe on her territory, some rough seas are in the forecast.

Made in the USA
Monee, IL
23 November 2021

82872254R00090